They Can See You

Fidel Monte

BMN Publishing

Contents

Prologue

The mountains were supposed to be silent. That was what the older priests promised when Mateo arrived at Santa Monica: silence for prayer, silence for healing, and silence for the voice of God. Yet on his first night in the seminary, the silence did not soothe him. It pressed against his skin like cold breath, as though the trees themselves were leaning close to listen.

He lay in the narrow bed of the Novitiate dormitory, eyes open in the dark, trying to steady his chest with slow breaths. The other novices had already surrendered to sleep, their breathing a steady rhythm. But Mateo could not. A strange weight lingered in the air, heavier than fatigue.

And then came certainty. He was being watched.

At first, he told himself it was the crucifix above the doorway, the soft outline of Christ's face lit by the moonlight that slid through the shutters. But no—this gaze was not gentle. It was piercing, unblinking, and relentless. Somewhere beyond the dormitory walls, or perhaps inside his very mind, something had fixed its eyes on him.

Mateo turned to the window. Outside, the path to the grotto cut through the trees, a silver thread under the moon. The grotto of the Blessed Virgin stood there at the gate of the seminary—he had passed it earlier, bowing quickly, almost fearfully. Now, in the stillness, he thought he saw the faintest shimmer of movement near the shadowy entrance of the grotto.

His body stiffened. His throat dried. He tried to whisper a prayer, but the words clung stubbornly to his tongue. All he could manage was the thought, sharp and cold:

"They can see me."

The sound of the bell drifted through his memory then—though no bell was ringing. A phantom toll echoed from San Agustin, dragging him back into the corridors of betrayal that he believed he had left behind. He pressed his palms to his face, but the feeling only grew stronger: not only was he remembered—he was exposed.

The silence was not empty after all. They were watching him.

Morning light broke through the mountains with a gentleness Mateo had almost forgotten. The mist rose from the valley like incense, and the pealing of the Angelus bell summoned the novices to prayer. To any outsider, the scene was holy, serene, and untouched by corruption.

Mateo forced himself into that rhythm: rise, wash, and join the others in the chapel. The chapel itself was small, built of stone and wood, its windows open to the forest. The priest who welcomed them, Fr. Ignacio, spoke softly in accented English about the MW way of life: listening to the Word, embracing simplicity, and living in brotherhood.

The other novices nodded eagerly, some even smiling. Mateo tried to mirror them, but his body betrayed him. His hands shook as he held the breviary. His heart raced with a nervousness that had no cause—unless he admitted the truth: the gaze from last night had followed him into daylight.

During the orientation, he stole glances at the door, at the windows, and at the shadows that pooled under the benches. There was no one there, of course. And yet, he felt the same unyielding pressure, like invisible eyes boring through his chest.

When the bell rang for breakfast, Mateo startled so violently that the novice beside him whispered, "First-day nerves?" Mateo forced a smile. He couldn't explain that the sound of bells, once the center of his obedience in San Agustin, now clawed at old scars—summoning not discipline, but dread.

After breakfast came the silence hour, where each novice was meant to meditate alone with Scripture. Mateo sat with the Bible open before him. The words blurred. He tried to focus on the verse: *The Lord is my shepherd; I shall not want.* But his gaze kept drifting to the window.

Outside, on the path to the grotto, the figure of the Virgin stood, carved in pale stone, framed by vines. Mateo blinked once—and froze. For a heartbeat, he was certain the statue was not alone. Something darker lingered beside her, half-hidden in shadow, as if standing guard.

A chill slid through him. He shut the Bible, clutching it like a shield. The bell rang again, soft and insistent.

And with it, a whisper rose in his memory, threading through the years of betrayal, echoing from voices he thought he had silenced:

We can still see you, Mateo.

CHAPTER I

Mountains of Santa Monica

The road that wound up in the mountains of Santa Monica seemed endless. Mateo sat in silence as the jeep rattled along the narrow path, each turn carving deeper into the fog and his uncertainty. He had left behind the diocesan seminary of San Agustin, with its bells, its rigid schedules, and its familiar walls of stone and manipulation. Now he faced something entirely different—not just a new seminary, but a new world.

The Novitiate of the Missionaries of the Word rose quietly at the end of the trail, framed by towering pine trees and hidden behind mist that never seemed to lift. From the very first sight, it carried an air of solemnity that was more unnerving than comforting. This was not a place of boys pretending at holiness, nor priests hiding corruption under the guise of tradition. This was something older, stricter, and more rooted in silence.

As Mateo entered, the first thing that struck him was the absence of noise. No chatter, no restless movements of seminarians jockeying for attention. The low chants of brothers reciting morning prayers filled the air, their voices flowing like a river of calm that Mateo could not yet step into.

The liturgy here felt heavier, weightier, almost like stone pressed upon his chest. The words were familiar—Psalms, readings, hymns—yet they carried a different force, as though every syllable had been carved out of centuries of devotion. And unlike San Agustin, where routine and the bell dictated every moment, here, prayer was not bound by duty but by intensity.

The Daily Rhythm

4:30 AM. The bell rang.

Not the sharp, commanding clang of San Agustin, but a hollow, resonant tone that seemed to echo inside the body. Mateo rose in darkness, fumbling into his habit, his body aching from the chill. Morning began not with words but with silence: the novices walked barefoot to the chapel, where candles already flickered in the shadows.

5:00 AM. Lauds.

Their voices rose together, chanting psalms in unison. The sound was haunting in the stillness of dawn, their words seeping into the wood and stone. Mateo's throat tightened as he tried to keep up, but the chants felt foreign, as though his own voice betrayed him.

6:00 AM. Meditation and Yoga.

They were led to the meditation hall, where mats were laid across the floor. Incense curled upward in slow, deliberate spirals. The novice master spoke little, only instructing, *"Sit. Breathe." Empty.* The exercises stretched the body, disciplined the breath, and pushed the mind toward stillness. Mateo's muscles trembled, his thoughts screamed, and instead of peace, he found only the ghosts of his past clawing louder.

7:00 AM. Eucharist.

Here, the Mass was not a hurried obligation but a deep immersion. Every gesture carried weight. The Word was proclaimed with such reverence that Mateo felt small beneath it, as though Scripture itself stood taller than the priest.

8:00 AM. Breakfast.

Silence continued. The meal was simple: rice, vegetables, bread, and a little fruit. No one spoke. Forks and spoons touched plates softly, as though even hunger was sacred. Mateo wanted to speak, to break the stillness with a word, but his voice remained trapped in his chest.

9:00 AM–11:00 AM. Lectio Divina.

In a long hall lined with bookshelves, each novice sat with a Bible, a journal, and silence. The practice was not to study but to listen—to let the Word pierce and dwell. Mateo read, but the words blurred. He scribbled thoughts, but doubt haunted him: *If the Word is salvation, why did those who carried it once destroy me?*

12:00 PM. Angelus. Lunch.

More silence. Occasionally, a reading was given aloud during meals: a passage from the Gospels or the words of the founder. Mateo chewed slowly, trying not to think about how foreign this rhythm was, how different from the noisy meals of his family long ago.

1:00 PM–4:00 PM. Manual Work.

In the gardens and fields, Mateo was assigned to clear weeds, plant seedlings, and carry water. The labor was physical, grounding, yet exhausting. Sweat stung his eyes.

The others worked in harmony, their movements steady and purposeful. Mateo lagged, his body unaccustomed, his mind wandering back to San Agustin, back to the bell, back to the faces of those he wanted to forget.

4:00 PM–6:00 PM. Study.

Lessons in spirituality, theology, homiletics, and the missionary charism. The lecturers spoke with burning conviction: *The Word of God is the only source of faith. The Word must be preached to the ends of the earth.* Mateo wrote notes obediently, but the words scratched against his soul. If the Word was everything, why had those who preached it wounded him most?

6:00 PM. Vespers.

A glow of sunset filled the chapel as they sang. For a moment, Mateo felt it—a flicker of beauty, of something beyond himself. Then it vanished.

7:00 PM. Dinner.

Silence again. The sound of spoons hitting the table fills the air. The hum of insects can be heard outside.

8:00 PM. Great Silence.

After Compline, the day ended with darkness. No words until dawn. Mateo lay in his narrow bed, eyes open, listening to the heavy breath of the novices around him. The silence pressed on him like a weight.

The first week blurred into one long meditation between despair and hope. Some mornings, he woke certain he had found his true home at last. Other days, the weight of discipline and the strangeness of yoga, chanting, and meditation made him wonder if he had stepped into something far more dangerous—not because of abuse or betrayal, but because the silence here forced him to face *himself*.

And in those moments, Mateo feared that what he might find within was more terrifying than anything Fr. Alvarez or Miss Lolita had ever done to him.

Chapter 2

Whispers in the Silence

The first week passed like a blur of discipline, silence, and aching muscles. By the second week, Mateo's body began to submit—rising at the bell without protest, kneeling on cold chapel floors until his knees numbed, and pulling weeds in the garden without complaint. The rhythm seeped into his bones.

But it was his mind that refused obedience.

The Great Silence was the hardest. From Compline until dawn, no word was spoken, no sound permitted but the breath of sleepers and the occasional creak of wood. At first, Mateo welcomed it, thinking silence would shield him from the chaos of memory. Instead, it became a mirror that reflected too much.

One night, as he lay in his narrow bed, staring into the dark rafters, he heard it—a faint whisper. At first he thought it was one of the novices murmuring in his sleep. But the sound was too close. It came not from the other beds, but from beside his own.

"Mateo..."

He froze. His breath caught in his throat. The name had been clear, soft, and almost intimate. He turned his head, but nothing moved in the blackness. His roommates breathed steadily, unbroken.

It happened again the following night. Then again. The same voice, never louder than a sigh, always calling his name.

During meditation, while the novices sat cross-legged in incense and stillness, Mateo sometimes felt the same presence behind him. A weight pressing just above his shoulder, as though someone leaned close, peering into his thoughts. Each time, he opened his eyes to find only the master pacing slowly, silently across the room.

And then, during Lectio Divina, as he traced his finger along the passage in John's Gospel—*The Word was made flesh, and dwelt among us*—the letters began to blur and shift. The ink trembled, forming shapes he could not name. For a moment, he thought the words themselves were bleeding into something else. He blinked hard, and they returned to normal.

Mateo told no one. How could he? The novices around him seemed at peace. Their silence was not torment but sanctuary. Only he struggled. Only he heard the whispers.

The Question of Faith

The novice master, Fr. Ignacio, was unlike any priest Mateo had ever known. His face was stern yet calm, his eyes piercing without cruelty. He never raised his voice, yet when he spoke, the words carried the weight of command.

One afternoon, after study, Fr. Ignacio paused beside Mateo's desk.

"You are restless," he said simply.

Mateo looked up, startled. "Father, I—"

"Your silence is not silence. It is noisy wearing a mask."

The words sank deep. Mateo lowered his gaze. He wanted to explain, to confess the whispers, the shifting words, and the shadows that moved where no shadows should. But something in him resisted. He feared being dismissed as weak—or worse, as broken beyond repair.

Instead, he muttered, "I am trying."

Fr. Ignacio studied him for a long moment. Then he said, "Silence does not hide the voice of God, Mateo. But neither does it hide the voice of your wounds."

The words unsettled him more than comforted him.

Nightfall

That evening, as the chapel emptied after Vespers, Mateo lingered. Candles flickered low, creating long shadows that covered the floor. He knelt alone, head bowed.

"Lord," he whispered under his breath, breaking the Great Silence for the first time. "If You are here, speak. If You are not... then let me go."

The air shifted. He felt it—a chill passing over his skin. And from the dark corner of the chapel, where the light did not reach, he thought he saw movement. A figure, robed and still, standing just beyond the last candle's glow.

He blinked. Gone.

Yet as he rose to leave, a whisper followed him, so close it brushed his ear.

"You will not escape."

The silence of Santa Monica was no longer empty. They were watching him.

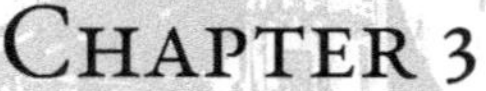

CHAPTER 3

Faces in the Shadows

Mateo began to dread the night. The Great Silence that others embraced had become his battlefield. Each time the bell tolled Compline, a coil of tension tightened inside his chest.

The third week, the whispers no longer came only at night. They began creeping into the hours of study and prayer. During Scripture reading, a voice would curl between the lines, weaving words that were not written. During meditation, when his eyes were closed, faces would surface in the darkness—half-formed but unmistakably familiar.

One morning, while hoeing weeds in the seminary garden, Mateo felt the sunlight darken. He looked up, sweat dripping from his brow. Between the rows of cassava, a figure stood watching him. Not a novice, not a priest.

It was Fr. Alvarez.

His cassock looked the same as when Mateo last saw him, but his face—his face was wrong. Hollow eyes, skin stretched too tight, a grin that lingered too long. Mateo dropped the hoe, heart pounding.

When he blinked, the figure was gone. Only the wind was moving through the cassava leaves.

The Cracks in Memory

He told himself it was memory. A wound resurfacing. But that evening, during meditation, another figure appeared.

This time, it was Miss Lolita.

She was seated across the room, though no women were permitted within the seminary walls. Her hair was perfectly coiled, her lips painted red, and her gaze fixed directly on him. No one else seemed to notice. The novices sat motionless, eyes closed, their breath steady in unison.

Mateo felt the old chill—the fear of her voice, her manipulation, and the weight of her control over his boyhood. He tried to shut his eyes, to banish her. But when he opened them again, she was closer. Sitting almost within reach.

And then, as if mocking him, she whispered the exact words she had once said to him when he was only a junior student at San Agustin High School:

"Mateo, you have to trust me. I would never do anything to harm you. I have always cared for you as if you were my own."

He gasped, breaking the silence, and the novices turned. But the space across from him was empty. Only the incense smoke was curling in the air.

Counsel of Silence

Fr. Ignacio summoned him after Lauds the next day.

"You are struggling again," the master said, his tone neither soft nor harsh, simply unyielding.

Mateo tried to speak, but his mouth was dry. At last he managed: "Father, I see things. I hear... them. Faces from the past."

Fr. Ignacio did not flinch. He folded his hands and asked, "Do you think they are real?"

"I don't know," Mateo admitted, trembling. "Sometimes I think I am losing my mind. Sometimes I think..." He stopped himself.

"Sometimes you think what?"

"That they followed me here."

The room fell into heavy silence. Then Fr. Ignacio said, "The walls of Santa Monica do not keep out demons, Mateo. They only strip away the noise so you can hear them more clearly. What you choose to do with that voice will ultimately determine who you become.

Mateo left shaken. The question gnawed at him: were these demons or simply the ghosts of his memory?

The Night of the Bell

That night, the seminary bell rang without cause. No feast day, no vigil. Just three slow tolls that woke the novices from their beds. Mateo sat upright, heart pounding. Unbeknownst to him, no one had rung the bell.

And in the darkness, a voice whispered once more. Not from the shadows this time, but from inside him.

"They can see you now."

CHAPTER 4

The Resistance

Mateo decided he would not let the shadows win. If Santa Monica had stripped him bare, then he would arm himself again—not with the weapons of the world, but with prayer, discipline, and the Word.

Each night after Compline, he stayed awake longer than the other novices. He read the Gospels by candlelight, forcing himself to linger over every verse. When the whispers came, he spoke the words aloud, louder and louder, until his throat was raw.

During meditation, when faces began to form in the dark, he clenched his fists and turned his breathing into a weapon. He remembered Fr. Ignacio's words: "The walls do not keep demons out. They only make you hear them."

So he told himself, "If I hear them, I can also silence them."

But the silence never lasted.

Scripture as Shield

One evening, he copied verses onto scraps of paper and placed them under his pillow, inside his shoes, and even taped to the walls of his cell.

"The Word became flesh and dwelt among us."

"The Lord is my light and my salvation; whom shall I fear?"

"Resist the devil, and he will flee from you."

He whispered them like incantations, hoping they would ward off the memories.

Yet the opposite happened.

When he lay down to sleep, the scraps under his pillow rustled, and in the rustling came a voice—Alvarez's voice—reading the very Scripture Mateo had written. The tone was mocking, each verse twisted until it sounded like an accusation.

And when he opened his eyes, the candle flame had not gone out but had burned taller, stretched thin, and black, as though the shadow itself had caught fire.

Mateo's body shook, and in panic he pressed the crucifix to his chest. "Leave me!" he shouted.

The flame snapped back to normal. The whispers stopped. But sleep never came.

The Yoga of Fear

The next morning, during yoga practice in the meditation hall, he tried to steady himself. The novices bent their bodies into silence: legs crossed, hands resting on their knees, eyes closed.

Mateo followed, inhaling the mountain air, exhaling the clutter. For a moment, he almost believed it was working—until he opened his eyes.

Across from him, where Julian sat in deep meditation, he saw her.

Miss Lolita.

Not in flesh, not fully formed. But her shape hovered like a double exposure over Julian's body, her smile stitched across his meditative stillness. And as Mateo stared, she turned her head—though Julian had not moved—and mouthed the words again:

"I would never do anything to harm you."

Mateo lurched out of position, breaking the circle. The others opened their eyes, startled, but saw only Julian sitting serenely.

Mateo's heart hammered. He knew now: the shadows did not come only at night.

Counsel of the Word

Desperate, he sought Fr. Ignacio again.

"I prayed harder. I wrote the Scriptures. I tried silence. I tried meditation. And still they come."

The master of novices looked at him long and hard. "Do you believe the Word is a weapon, Mateo?"

"Yes," Mateo answered without hesitation.

Ignacio leaned closer. "It is not. The Word is not meant to be swung like a sword. It is meant to pierce you. To change you. It cannot survive inside until what is false is removed.

"But if they are real…" Mateo whispered, voice breaking.

"If they are real," Ignacio said, "then they know your fear better than you do."

The Escalation

That night, Mateo tried a new resolve: he would not speak, not resist, not cry out. If the shadows came, he would let them.

And they did.

The bell tolled again at midnight, though no brother touched the rope. The novices stirred in their sleep, restless but unaware.

Mateo sat upright. At the foot of his bed stood Fr. Alvarez, his hollow face gleaming in the moonlight. Behind him, half-hidden in the corner, Miss Lolita waited, her painted lips curving into that poisonous smile.

This time, they did not speak.

They only stared.

And as Mateo gripped the crucifix to his chest, a new terror sank into him: what if they were not coming from outside at all—but from within him, rising with each breath he took?

CHAPTER 5

The Choir

The first hints of December crept into Santa Monica through the cold wind that rattled the pine trees and sharpened the mountain air. With the season came a sense of expectation. For weeks, the brothers spoke of the General Christmas Celebration—a gathering where each seminary house would present music, drama, or prayer at the main auditorium. It was tradition, but more than that, it was pride.

This year, the Music Director sought something stronger than routine hymns. He wanted a choir that could stand out, that could lift the mountain walls with harmony. And so he looked to Mateo.

A Hidden Gift

Mateo had not advertised his talent. His music skills had first drawn attention in the chapel, where he sang without effort, pure and steady, while playing the guitar at the same time. During recreation, when brothers hummed familiar tunes, he instinctively found the second voice, weaving harmony that made even simple melodies seem richer.

"Brother Mateo," the Director said one afternoon after Vespers, "I want you to form a choir. You'll lead the novices and train them. Can you handle it?"

Mateo hesitated. Leadership was not what he had come here for. He wanted silence, healing, and invisibility. Yet the Director's gaze was firm, almost fatherly.

"Yes, Father," Mateo answered.

Gathering Voices

The next day, he called the novices to the music room. The air smelled of dust and wood polish; the old piano sat against the wall like a forgotten relic.

"Some of you can sing," Mateo said simply. "Some of you think you can't. But everyone will try."

He divided them by range: tenor 1, tenor 2, bass 1, and bass 2. Julian, eager and bright, was placed among the tenors. Others grumbled, but curiosity kept them there.

When they sang their first hymn together, the result was chaos—off-key, uneven, with laughter cutting through the solemnity. But Mateo only smiled faintly. "Again," he said.

And again they sang.

Discipline Through Song

What struck him was how much choir practice mirrored seminary life: repetition, obedience, and silence between commands. He taught them to listen to one another, to match pitches, and to breathe as one.

"Your voice is not yours alone," he reminded them. "It belongs to the body. To the whole."

At first, they resisted. But gradually, something shifted. Their voices blended. Their breathing fell in rhythm. Even the roughest singers began to find their place.

Music was shaping them—and Mateo felt himself being shaped too.

The Shadow in the Harmony

Yet in moments of beauty, shadows still intruded.

One evening, as they practiced the Gloria in Excelsis Deo, the sound rose so high it seemed to shake the windows. Mateo closed his eyes, almost transported.

Then he heard it. A voice not among them—low, mocking, dissonant. It slipped through the harmony like poison.

"You sing beautifully, Mateo," the voice drawled, unmistakably Alvarez's. "But do you know whose choir you really lead?"

Mateo's eyes flew open. The novices sang on, oblivious. Not one of them seemed to hear the extra voice.

He swallowed hard and forced himself to keep conducting.

Hope in the Sound

Despite the intrusion, the choir improved. Day by day, their sound grew fuller, richer, and more confident. And Mateo, though shaken, felt something stirring within him. For the first time since coming to Santa Monica, he was not only enduring. He was creating.

The Music Director noticed. "They follow you well," he said after rehearsal. "There is strength in your hands, Mateo. Do not forget that."

Strength. Mateo repeated the word silently. Perhaps music was more than escape. Perhaps it was a weapon, one the shadows could not fully corrupt.

Toward the Celebration

As the day of the Christmas gathering drew nearer, anticipation spread through the novices. They sang at dawn, at dusk, until their throats ached and their hearts beat to the rhythm of carols.

And Mateo, standing at the center, could not help but wonder:

Would their music rise above the whispers—or would the darkness find a way to join the chorus?

CHAPTER 6

The Carols

The first Advent candle had barely been lit when the Music Director gathered the choir in the small rehearsal hall and announced, "This year, we will not only sing at the General Christmas Celebration. We will go out to the neighboring seminaries, to the convents, and to the villages. We will bring carols into the streets."

A murmur of excitement swept through the novices. To leave the mountain walls, even briefly, felt like stepping into another world. For some, it was simply the thrill of travel; for others, it was the chance to taste mission, to sing where faith was less rehearsed, more raw.

Mateo stood quietly, his eyes lowered. He understood the Director's intent: music was not just for ornament. It was a proclamation. It was subtle evangelization. The Word clothed in melody.

A Campus of Many Orders

Santa Monica was not only home to the Missionaries of the Word. Scattered across the slopes and valleys were houses of other orders—Jesuits with their rigorous studies, Benedictines with their silence and order, Carmelites wrapped in contemplation, and several communities of sisters, each with their own rhythm of prayer and work.

It was agreed that the choir would begin their caroling here, among their brothers and sisters in formation. "To sing for them is to remind them that we walk together," the Director explained.

The first night, they filed into the Carmelite chapel, the novices in black habits looking on in silence. When the choir began Silent Night, their voices seemed to hang in the still air, blending with the incense. One of the nuns wept quietly, her face hidden behind her veil.

"Your song," the Prioress told them afterward, "was prayer itself."

Mateo bowed, humbled.

Villages in the Valley

Soon, they descended into the villages scattered along the mountain roads. The townspeople greeted them with wide eyes and warm smiles, some children clutching their mothers' skirts in awe at the sight of seminarians in cassocks.

They sang before houses lit by oil lamps, their carols echoing into the night. At one home, an old woman pressed Mateo's hands. "You remind us of God's nearness," she whispered. "Don't ever stop."

Word spread quickly: the Missionaries of the Word had come singing. Crowds began to gather wherever they went. For the villagers, the carols were not just music; they were living reminders of a God who still walked with them in the quiet, in the cold, and in the small forgotten corners of the earth.

And for the seminary, the caroling became a subtle invitation: Perhaps you, too, young man, are called to this life. Perhaps you, too, can sing the Word to the ends of the earth.

The Other Seminaries

One evening, the choir visited a neighboring formation house of the Franciscans. Their chapel was simple, the brothers barefoot, their brown habits frayed. After the carol, the Franciscan novice master smiled.

"You sing of heaven," he said. "But remember, the poor must also hear this song. Do not keep it only for chapels and towns."

The words struck Mateo deeply. He had always seen music as a refuge, but here it was being drawn into something larger, more demanding: a mission.

A Growing Fire

The nights of caroling became a rhythm of their own—singing, walking, and laughing quietly under the stars. Julian often stayed close to Mateo, his tenor voice steady at his side. "You were meant for this," he told him once after a long evening. "Not just to hide. To lead."

Mateo did not answer. His heart was torn between the comfort of music and the shadow of voices that lingered at the edge of every hymn.

But something undeniable was happening. Wherever the choir sang, light seemed to kindle—in the eyes of children, in the tears of nuns, and in the solemn nods of fellow seminarians.

It was as though the Word itself was finding new soil, carried on the breath of carols.

Shadows Between Songs

And yet, the shadows did not vanish.

One night, after a triumphant carolling in a nearby town, the novices walked back up the mountain path, their lanterns flickering in the wind. Mateo lingered behind, savoring the silence.

That was when he heard it—a faint humming, just beyond his shoulder. The tune was familiar: O Come, O Come Emmanuel. But it was twisted, slow, and almost mocking.

He turned quickly. No one was there. Only the dark road winding into the trees.

The others had gone ahead, their laughter fading. Mateo stood alone, the cold air pressing against his chest.

The voice whispered low, almost tender: "You can sing, Mateo. But do you really believe the One you sing of?"

He froze. His lantern flickered. Then he forced his feet to move faster until he rejoined the group.

He said nothing. But the echo of the question stayed with him.

Toward the Celebration

Caroling became the heartbeat of Advent in Santa Monica. The choir's reputation spread; the Music Director smiled more often now, and even the Rector nodded approvingly when they passed.

But Mateo knew the true test was yet to come: the General Christmas Celebration at the main auditorium, where all houses of formation would gather.

Would their music still carry light before such a crowd?

Or would the shadows seize the chance to sing along?

Chapter 7

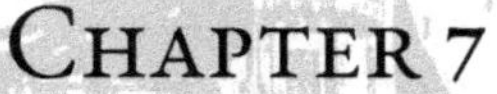

The Restless Night

Advent at Santa Monica was usually marked by candles and quiet prayer, a season of longing and expectation. But for Mateo, longing had twisted into dread.

Each day, rehearsals grew more intense as the celebration drew nearer. The choir's harmonies grew fuller, their confidence stronger, and their sound ready to fill the great auditorium. The other novices laughed in relief after long sessions, their spirits lifted by the joy of song.

But when night fell, Mateo's peace unraveled.

The Weight of Silence

In the darkness of his cell, silence was never quiet. The echoes came. Sometimes it was just a murmur; other times, a full chorus of mockery. The more he prayed, the more it felt as though something laughed back at him from the shadows.

He sat on his cot one midnight, head buried in his hands. His candle had long burned out, but sleep would not come. "Why sing, Mateo?" the voice teased. "Do you not see? Your voice betrays you. It will betray you on that stage."

He pressed his palms firmly against his ears until they ached. But the whispers came from within, not without.

The Fear of Unmasking

As the celebration loomed, Mateo's fear sharpened into a single image: that he would stand before the gathered orders, the sisters, the novices, and the priests, and suddenly—his voice would falter. Or worse, that another voice would rise through his throat, something not his own.

The thought paralyzed him.

By day, his leadership in rehearsals drew admiration. By night, he saw only the possibility of shame. The choir trusted him and depended on his cues and his steadiness. If he faltered, all would falter.

"Lord," he whispered one evening in the chapel after compline, "do not let me be their downfall." His words trembled on the cold marble floor.

Julian's Watchful Eyes

Julian noticed. He always did.

"You're pale," he said one afternoon after practice. "You hardly sleep, do you?"

Mateo forced a laugh. "It's nothing. Just… nerves."

But Julian's eyes lingered, sharp, probing. "You're afraid of more than music. I can see it."

Mateo turned away, unable to meet his gaze. To speak the truth aloud felt too dangerous, as if voicing it would give the shadows more power.

The Advent Wreath

On the third Sunday, the rose candle was lit. The choir sang "Gaudete," their voices ringing with joy. But for Mateo, the hymn's call to rejoice felt hollow, like a bell with a crack.

During Mass, as the choir sang, he caught sight of a flicker in the sanctuary corner—a shadow darker than the rest, lingering too long, watching. When he blinked, it was gone. But the taste of fear stayed in his mouth like iron.

A Quiet Warning

That night, in the refectory, the Rector spoke during dinner. His words were meant as encouragement, but to Mateo, they carried another weight.

"Remember, young men," the Rector said, "when you stand before the world, you do not stand for yourselves. You stand for Him. If you falter, falter in Him. If you triumph, triumph in Him. But never forget—evil, too, wishes to sing. Be vigilant."

The hall grew still. Mateo's spoon froze in his hand.

It was as though the Rector had spoken directly to his secret terror. His chest tightened. Could the Rector know?

The Sleepless Vigil

That night, Mateo did not even try to sleep. He sat by the small window, staring at the mountain ridge. The wind howled softly, like a distant chant. His breath came shallow and uneven.

What if it happens? he thought. What if before them all, the darkness unmasks itself through me?

His hands trembled. The shadows in his room seemed to swell, pressing closer, as if waiting.

Mateo knelt suddenly, his knees striking the stone floor. "Lord!" he cried in a hoarse whisper. "Do not let them see me fall. Not in front of them. Not in front of You."

But the silence that followed felt heavier than any answer.

And in that silence, he sensed it—not words, not sound, but a presence. Patient. Watching. Almost amused.

The celebration was only days away. And Mateo knew: something would come. It was something he had never anticipated.

CHAPTER 8

The Christmas Celebration

The great auditorium of Santa Monica gleamed with light. Wreaths of pine and ribbons of gold framed the stage, while the Advent wreath stood tall at the center, its candles glowing against the velvet backdrop. The air was rich with the mingling scents of wax, pine, and incense that had drifted in from the afternoon Mass.

The Christmas Celebration was more than a concert; it was a gathering of the Church's young. Seminarians from every house, novices from the different orders, and sisters from the neighboring convents—all were present, their faces bright with anticipation. Even townsfolk had been invited, filling the back rows of the auditorium with a hum of eager voices.

Tonight, Santa Monica would display not only its devotion but also its pride. And at the heart of it stood the choirs.

A Festival of Voices

One by one, the choirs took the stage.

The Benedictine novices sang a haunting "Veni Emmanuel" that left the audience in reverent silence before erupting into applause. The Franciscan seminarians followed with a jubilant rendition of "Angels We Have Heard on High," and their voices soared like trumpets. The Dominican brothers surprised everyone with a folk-inspired carol from the mountains, their harmony accompanied by simple bamboo flutes, earning cheers and claps in rhythm.

With each performance, the audience leaned closer, their hands warming in applause, their hearts lifted in the shared joy of Christmas.

Mateo sat among his choir, dressed in their cream-white cassocks with golden sashes, his hands folded tightly on his lap. He smiled when his brothers nudged him, their faces flushed with excitement. But inside, a storm brewed.

Hold steady, he told himself. Your turn will come soon. Lead them well. Do not falter.

The Intermission

After the sixth choir, the emcee announced a brief intermission. The lights rose slightly, and the audience relaxed, murmuring with excitement over what they had heard so far. Some of the seminarians stretched their legs; others rushed for water.

Mateo tried to do the same—he rose, forcing a calm expression, and walked with Julian toward the side corridor. His chest tightened with every breath, but Julian's steady presence kept him from unraveling completely.

"You'll be fine," Julian whispered, placing a hand on his shoulder. "You've prepared them well. This will be Santa Monica's night."

Mateo nodded weakly. Yes. Santa Monica's night. Not mine.

The Announcement

Then, just as the audience was settling back in, the Music director—an older priest with sharp eyes and a booming voice—walked to the podium. He adjusted the microphone, his cassock sweeping against the wooden floor.

"Brothers and sisters," he began, his voice echoing across the auditorium, "what a blessed evening this has been. We have witnessed the joy of Christ proclaimed in song, the beauty of our faith carried on the wings of harmony."

Applause rose again, warm and grateful. The Director raised a hand for silence.

"But before we close tonight's celebration," he continued, "we have a special gift." His eyes gleamed. "Our final performance will come not from our resident choirs, but from guests who have traveled far to be with us. They come from the Diocese of San Agustin—a choir well-known across the region, beloved for their dedication and excellence. They recently won the national grand champion trophy during the national choral competition at the national choral center. Brothers and sisters, please give a warm Santa Monica mountains welcome to the Diocesan Choir of San Agustin, under the direction of their Choir Master, Father Alvarez!"

The hall erupted in applause, cheers bouncing off the high ceiling. The audience stood in ovation as the visiting choir filed in from the wings.

Mateo's Collapse

Mateo did not stand. His legs locked, his vision blurred. For a moment he thought the floor had given way beneath him. His breath caught in his throat, shallow and ragged.

San Agustin.

The name struck him like a blow. His chest clenched, his heart pounding in painful bursts. Faces flashed before his eyes—the streets of his childhood, the parish bells, and the eyes that had once known him. And then, most terrifying of all: Father Alvarez.

He felt as if he had died in that instant. He wanted to. He wished for anything that would spare him from the collision of his two worlds.

Julian's hand gripped his arm. "Mateo!" he whispered urgently. "Sit down. Breathe!"

But Mateo could not move, could not think. The hall around him blurred in light and shadow. The applause sounded distant and distorted, as though underwater.

The Entrance of the Past

The Diocesan Choir mounted the stage in disciplined lines, their cassocks crisp, their faces bright with pride. At their front walked a tall, broad-shouldered priest, his silver hair catching the stage light. Father Alvarez. His presence commanded the room, dignified and calm, his every step measured.

For Mateo, it was as if the walls themselves were closing in.

He clutched at the bench, nails digging into the wood. No. Not here. Not now. Please, God, not him.

The visiting choir bowed. The audience roared with approval. Father Alvarez raised his hand, and at once, silence fell—the kind of silence that belongs only to a master of music and souls.

A Song from Home

The choir began.

It was not just any carol. It was the old hymn of San Agustin, the one sung every Christmas Eve in the parish church, the one that had once carried Mateo's boyhood voice through the nave like a bright thread of hope.

Hearing it now, in this place, tore him open.

He gripped his chest. The melody stabbed at old wounds—memories of home, of belonging, of pain too deep to name. Each note was a reminder of everything he had fled, everything he thought was buried.

His breath came faster, his vision swimming. He could almost hear another voice whispering inside him: "They are here for you. You cannot escape."

The Clash Within

Julian leaned close, whispering urgently. "Mateo, what's wrong? Tell me—"

But Mateo shook his head violently. His throat was locked, words impossible.

He wanted to run, to flee the hall, but his body betrayed him. He was frozen, caught between the beauty of the song and the terror of recognition.

Would Father Alvarez see him? Would one of the choristers glance his way and remember? If their eyes met, what truth would spill out on this holy night?

Mateo pressed his hands to his ears, but it was no use. The hymn burrowed deeper, a song that was no longer just music but memory, judgment, and fear entwined.

The Standing Ovation

When the final chord rang and fell into silence, the hall erupted again, this time in thunderous applause. The audience rose to their feet, clapping and cheering with abandon. Some shouted, "Bravo!" Others wiped tears from their eyes.

Father Alvarez bowed, smiling and gracious, as the Diocesan Choir stood proud behind him.

And in the chaos of celebration, Mateo sat trembling, his cassock damp with sweat, his face pale as linen. He had not clapped, had not moved. Only his eyes, fixed on the stage, betrayed the storm within.

In that moment, he realized that the past he believed he had left behind had caught up with him again.

And there would be no hiding now.

CHAPTER 9

The Shadow That Followed

The applause was still echoing in the great hall when Mateo felt a cold presence wrap around him, one that no warmth of Christmas could melt. His choir companions laughed and chatted, still caught in the glow of their performance, while he stood stiff, waiting for the inevitable.

Then, it came.

"Mateo," a voice said from behind.

He turned slowly, already knowing. Fr. Alvarez stood there, draped not just in his clerical robes but in the authority he always carried like a second skin. His eyes bored into Mateo with that same piercing intensity that once commanded obedience. The years, the distance—none of it had dulled the power he held over him.

"Can we talk? Just a few minutes," Fr. Alvarez asked. But it was not a request. It was an order disguised in politeness.

Mateo's heart screamed to say no, to refuse, to run back to the safety of his brothers. But fear caught him by the throat, pressing down like a hand over his mouth. He nodded.

They stepped away from the crowd into a quieter corner, where the soft glow of Christmas lights did little to soften the darkness between them. Fr. Alvarez wasted no time.

"Why did you leave me?" His tone was sharp, wounded pride wrapped in anger. "Why did you abandon your opportunity to become my successor? I trained you. I guided you. I molded you." He leaned closer, his voice lowering to a hiss. "And you just left me?"

Mateo stood frozen. He wanted to speak, to explain that he left because he wanted freedom, because he was searching for God—not a prison built from one man's control. But no words came. His lips parted, and yet nothing emerged. His silence only fed Alvarez's fury.

"I want you to come back, Mateo." Alvarez's hand gripped his shoulder, firm and possessive. "You belong with me. With us. Not here in these mountains, wasting your potential among strangers."

Mateo tried to step back, but the grip tightened. Alvarez's voice darkened, carrying a weight Mateo had known too well.

"Remember this, Mateo," he said slowly, each word deliberate, like the toll of a bell of doom. "I will do everything in my power so you will come back to me."

The words cut deep, colder than the December air. Alvarez released him and, without waiting for a response, turned and walked back to his choir, blending once again into the celebration as though nothing had happened.

Mateo was left standing in the shadows, trembling. His throat felt tight, his chest heavy, and his whole body paralyzed. The voices rose in joy as the carols resumed, but the echo of Alvarez's threat drowned out the music for Mateo.

He found himself unable to move. He couldn't breathe. He couldn't even pray.

In that moment, the great hall felt smaller than the San Agustin seminary walls, and he realized with horror that no matter how far he had run, Alvarez had found him.

Chapter 10
Another Restless Night

The celebration wound down with fireworks and cheers echoing across the mountain compound. The smell of roasted chestnuts, pine, and melted wax lingered in the air. Novices, priests, and nuns mingled joyfully, their voices bright and untroubled. But Mateo drifted through the festivity like a ghost, a hollow figure wrapped in silence.

He forced smiles when spoken to, nodded when congratulated, and even sang along when one of the brothers began a spontaneous round of "O Come, All Ye Faithful." But his mind was elsewhere—still trapped in that corner of the auditorium where Fr. Alvarez's grip had burned into his shoulder, where the words still rang like a curse: "I will do everything in my power so you will come back to me."

When the celebration ended and the novices marched back to the seminary in single file, Mateo lagged behind. The mountain air was crisp, the stars scattered across the sky like spilled salt, but none of it comforted him. Every step echoed, every tree seemed to lean in, and he kept glancing over his shoulder, half-expecting Alvarez to be there, lurking just a few paces behind.

The dormitory was hushed that night, the glow of candles flickering on wooden walls. Most of the novices were too worn out to stay awake after the long day. Some prayed briefly before collapsing into their beds; others whispered stories until their voices trailed off into sleep. Mateo lay on his cot, staring up at the ceiling beams.

Sleep would not come.

Every time he closed his eyes, he saw Alvarez's face—stern, commanding, disappointed, and angry all at once. He remembered those days in San Agustin when Alvarez's approval had meant everything, when a single nod from him felt like grace itself. And yet, underneath that admiration had always been fear.

Now, in the silence of the night, that fear returned with greater force than ever.

He tossed and turned. The blanket felt too heavy. His breaths came shallow and quick. He whispered a prayer—half plea, half desperate attempt to drown out the voice in his head:

"Deliver me, Lord, from the hand of my enemies…"

But the words trailed off. A chill crept through the room, though the shutters were closed.

Then came the sound.

At first, Mateo thought it was the wind rattling the old windows. But it was too steady, too deliberate: footsteps in the corridor outside. Slow. Heavy. Dragging.

Mateo's body stiffened. His ears strained. No one should be walking the halls at this hour. The prefect had retired, and all the brothers were asleep. The sound came closer, pausing right outside his door.

He held his breath.

The doorknob turned—just slightly, as if someone tested it.

Mateo sat upright, heart pounding so loud he feared it would wake the others. But the door didn't open. After a few seconds, the footsteps resumed, fading slowly into the distance, swallowed by the silence.

Mateo wanted to dismiss it as imagination, the trick of an exhausted mind. But he knew better. He knew the sound of footsteps too well—the way

Alvarez used to pace the halls of San Agustin, making his presence known, reminding everyone that he was always near.

Sleep became impossible. He sat at the edge of his bed, head buried in his hands. The room felt smaller, the walls pressing in. He thought about running away—escaping far beyond Santa Monica and leaving everything behind. But where would he go? Alvarez had found him once; he could find him again.

The words returned, relentless, whispering in his skull: "I will do everything in my power so you will come back to me."

Mateo shuddered. Was Alvarez still here in Santa Monica, waiting? Or worse—was it not Alvarez at all, but something darker, using his voice and his image to torment him?

He tried to pray again, louder this time, enough to keep the fear at bay. "The Lord is my shepherd; I shall not want..." His lips trembled as he recited Psalm 23. But the peace that Scripture usually brought him was absent. Each verse felt like sand slipping through his fingers.

By dawn, Mateo had not slept a single moment. His eyes were red, his body drained, but his soul carried a greater weight: the terror that no matter how far he ran, the shadow of Alvarez would always follow him.

CHAPTER II

The 30-Day Retreat

After Christmas, the days at Santa Monica seemed to hang in a fragile quiet. Outwardly, nothing had changed. The novices still rose with the first bell, gathered in the dim chapel for prayer, and moved about the fields in a steady rhythm. But within Mateo, the world was different.

Ever since his encounter with Fr. Alvarez, the silence between the prayers had become heavier, almost unbearable. In those spaces, his thoughts no longer rested. His mind was restless, filled with whispers, and his chest tightened with fear of being seen through. He was haunted not by what others knew, but by what they might discover.

It was during this uneasy time that Fr. Ignacio, the Novice Master of the Missionaries of the Word, called the community together. His tone was measured, his voice carrying the weight of authority seasoned with calm.

"My sons," he began, standing before the assembled novices in the chapter hall, "you have walked nearly a year in this holy house. You have endured the test of daily prayer, manual labor, silence, and obedience. But before you continue into Philosophy and the long years of formation that lie ahead, you must first pass through the gate that will either strengthen or undo your vocation."

He paused, letting his words settle in the room.

"In two weeks' time, you will depart from Santa Monica to the mountains. There you will enter the thirty-day retreat. This retreat is modeled after the Spiritual Exercises of St. Ignatius of Loyola, which our order has adopted for the novitiate stage. For thirty days, you will live in silence, pray, and examine your soul. There will be no distractions, no worldly noises—only the voice of God, speaking in the quiet of your heart. It is a compulsory part of your formation. Only those who endure it truthfully will continue to the next stage of their calling."

The novices bowed their heads respectfully. A quiet murmur of "Deo gratias" followed. Anticipation filled many eyes; they spoke reverently about this retreat, describing it as the crucible that forged clarity of vocation.

Mateo, however, felt a chill crawl up his spine. Thirty days of silence. Thirty days without escape. He wondered, with a sinking dread, whether this retreat would strip him bare before God—or expose him to something far darker.

The journey to the retreat house began at dawn. The novices traveled by cart and foot, the road winding higher into the mountains. With each mile, the air grew thinner, the forests denser, and the world quieter. Mateo walked near the rear of the group, weighed down not only by the climb but also by an invisible burden that pressed harder with each step.

On the second evening, the retreat house finally appeared: a severe stone building clinging to the ridge, its cross rising against the bleeding horizon. It was simple, austere, and unsettlingly still. The silence there was not ordinary silence—it was thick, as if the very air forbade casual speech.

That night, Fr. Ignacio addressed them again in the chapel, his face lit only by the dim light of candles.

"From tomorrow," he said firmly, "your retreat begins. For thirty days, you will speak to no one but God. Every movement, every breath, every thought must be directed to Him. You will follow the Exercises with faith and discipline. The silence is not meant to burden you—it is meant to free you, to strip away the noise of the world. Some of you will find peace. Others may encounter restlessness, even resistance. But all of you will face yourselves. That is the way of God."

Mateo felt his stomach twist. Restlessness. Resistance. Those words clung to him as if they were chosen for him alone.

The silence began the next morning.

From that first dawn, the house became a tomb of quiet. Meals were taken without words, the scrape of spoons against bowls the loudest sound. Hours were spent in meditation and guided reflections from the Exercises, followed by long stretches of solitude. The novices' footsteps echoed in the stone halls as if magnified, each sound startling in its clarity.

For some, the silence was a balm; it sank into their bones like peace. But for Mateo, it was suffocating.

On the third night, as he prayed in his narrow cell, the candlelight flickering weakly, he heard it again—footsteps. Slow, deliberate pacing just outside his door. His grip on the rosary tightened until the beads cut into his skin.

Then, a whisper—faint, almost indistinguishable from the moan of the wind:

"Why did you leave me?"

His heart hammered in his chest. He leapt up and flung open the door. The corridor was empty, the shadows long and still. Nothing but cold stone.

Yet Mateo knew. Whether born of imagination, memory, or spirit, Alvarez's voice had followed him even here, to the silence of the mountains. And in this retreat—stripped of distraction, confined within silence—there was nowhere left to run.

CHAPTER 12

The Silence of the Mountains

Fr. Ignacio, the Novice Master of the Missionaries of the Word, presided over the retreat. His instruction was clear: the retreat was no ordinary time of prayer. "You will spend these days in great silence," Fr. Ignacio told them again in the chapel. "You will pray, you will reflect, and you will face God without excuses. If He desires you to remain, He will strengthen you. If He does not, He will show it clearly. There is no greater clarity than what silence reveals."

Mateo bowed his head with the others, but inside his chest, dread stirred.

Week One: The Weight of Sin

The first week plunged them into meditations on sin, death, judgment, and hell. Each day, the novices were instructed to consider their own lives in the light of eternity.

For Mateo, this week was unbearable. As he prayed alone in his cell, the words of the meditations twisted in his mind: the stench of sin, the flames of hell, and the loneliness of eternal separation. His rosary beads slipped from his fingers more than once as whispers returned in the silence.

At night, he heard them again—footsteps, pacing outside his cell. Sometimes he thought he saw the shadow of a man pass across his doorframe, though no novice was permitted to walk at such an hour. And once, faint but undeniable, he heard a voice murmur:

"You cannot hide forever."

His chest burned with shame. Was it his conscience? Or was it Alvarez's ghost that had followed him even into this holy silence?

Week Two: The Life of Christ

In the second week, the meditations shifted to the public life of Christ: His calling of the disciples, His miracles, and His compassion. The novices were told to imagine themselves walking beside Christ, seeing Him, hearing Him, and choosing to follow Him.

For most of the novices, this week brought lightness. Faces softened; some wept in their private prayers at the closeness they felt to the Lord. But Mateo could not escape the shadows that pressed against him.

When he imagined Christ calling the disciples by name, he felt the words snag in his heart. What if Christ called everyone—except me?

During meditation, his body sometimes trembled with a strange, oppressive fear. His eyes grew restless, darting even during the stillness of the chapel. And though he longed to pray, his prayers' words often turned dry on his tongue.

It was as though a wall had risen between himself and God, and on the other side of that wall was something waiting to accuse him.

Week Three: The Passion of Christ

The third week was the most severe. The novices entered into daily meditations on the Passion—the betrayal, the scourging, the carrying of the Cross, and the crucifixion.

For Mateo, the images of Christ's suffering cut deeply into his mind. He lingered on the themes of betrayal and denial, unable to escape the feeling that his very presence in the house of God was itself a betrayal. He felt restless at meals, his hands trembling as he lifted bread to his lips. In chapel, he shifted in his seat, unable to settle.

The silence of the mountain, once oppressive, now became almost unbearable. At times, Mateo pressed his palms to his ears as though to block out a sound that came from nowhere.

It was in this week that Fr. Ignacio noticed him most keenly.

The Confessor's Question

On the evening of the twenty-first day, as the sun bled red into the horizon and the mountains darkened into shadow, Fr. Ignacio approached Mateo.

They stood at the edge of the chapel, alone. The Novice Master's face was grave but calm.

"Mateo," he said quietly, "you have been very restless these past weeks. I see it in your eyes, in the way you cannot sit still at prayer, in the way silence burdens you."

Mateo lowered his head, his throat tightening.

Fr. Ignacio's tone softened, yet carried a peculiar weight. "I ask you plainly—do you need the sacrament of confession? It seems as though something is eating you inside."

Mateo hesitated, sensing something beneath the question. It was not merely an offer of mercy; it was an invitation into scrutiny. The words carried intent, almost as if they were not born solely from Fr. Ignacio's observation.

The way the priest's eyes held him, Mateo felt the unspoken pressure: *someone has told him to ask. Someone believes this is where they will uncover me—the real Mateo Aragon. And if they do, they will know whether I am fit to remain here at all.*

His stomach twisted. His palms grew damp. The silence between them stretched, heavy, suffocating.

Mateo opened his mouth, but no words came.

The Confession

Mateo's chest rose and fell as if he were standing before a cliff's edge. For a moment, he considered deflecting and admitting only the superficial sins that any novice could identify—such as impatience, distraction, and doubts in prayer. But then, against the tightening fear in his throat, he whispered:

"Yes, Father… I need confession."

Fr. Ignacio nodded and led him into the small chapel, where the flickering sanctuary lamp glowed red against the shadows. They knelt at the communion rail—one on either side.

Mateo's voice shook as he began the ritual words. Then, haltingly, he told the story.

He spoke of his junior year at San Agustin, of Miss Lolita, and of the confusing and sorrowful bond that had pulled him into shame. His words came tangled, full of hesitations, yet the weight behind them was unmistakable. He spoke not with detail but with pain—the pain of a boy who wanted to be pure yet found himself marked by something he could not forget.

"I don't even know," Mateo whispered, his hands clutching the wood of the rail, "if it was sin, or temptation, or weakness… all I know is that it has followed me. It's as though I am not clean enough to stand here, Father. As though I wear a stain that will not wash away."

The silence after his words was unbearable. The mountain wind whistled faintly against the chapel windows.

At last, Fr. Ignacio spoke, his voice calm, even gentle. "The mercy of Christ is greater than your past, Mateo. It is greater than any weakness, any shame, or any confusion of the heart. In the name of the Father, and of the Son, and of the Holy Spirit, I absolve you of your sins. Go in peace."

Relief washed through Mateo, sudden and sharp, like a flood bursting through a cracked dam. He trembled, tears burning his eyes. For the first time in weeks, his chest felt lighter, as though the silence itself had loosened its grip.

But then, as Mateo prepared to rise, Fr. Ignacio added words that froze him where he knelt.

The Puzzling Counsel

"Mateo," Fr. Ignacio said slowly, "you are gifted with prayer. You also have wounds that run deep. And sometimes… the order of a missionary is not where such wounds are best carried. Perhaps it is God's will that you continue not here, but at the diocesan seminary where you began. It may be there, not here, that your vocation is to be tested and formed."

Mateo's breath caught. His body stiffened. The words rang in his ears like a verdict.

The diocesan seminary. Not the Missionaries. Not the life he had given himself to.

A tremor ran through his limbs. In that instant, it was as though the shadows of the past rose and took shape before him. He remembered Alvarez's face, pale in the dim light, his voice curling like smoke:

"You will never be fit. Not here. Not anywhere."

And now—here it was again. The same judgment, but in the mouth of Fr. Ignacio.

Mateo's stomach turned cold. His knees pressed harder into the wood. He could not move.

For a long moment, he stared at the flickering sanctuary lamp, his thoughts a blur of disbelief and dread. He had trusted God. He had unburdened his heart. And yet the words of judgment had come back, sharpened, clothed in the very voice of authority.

His lips parted, but no sound emerged. The silence of the mountains pressed in, heavier than ever.

The Unbearable Silence

Mateo remained on his knees, unable to rise, the polished wood of the rail pressing into his flesh. His whole body trembled as though the earth beneath the chapel were shifting. The words of absolution still hung in the air, a promise of mercy. But louder—deeper—was the echo of rejection that had followed him through the years.

Santa Ana. The narrow streets, the childhood wounds he never spoke of.
San Agustin. The confusion, the shadow of Miss Lolita that had stained his youth.

The diocesan seminary. The restless nights of doubt, the feeling of not belonging.

And now—here, in the mountain silence of Santa Monica's retreat house—Fr. Ignacio's counsel, echoing Alvarez like a curse.

His hands clenched tight, nails digging into his palms. Sorrow welled up in him like a storm. Anger, too—hot, bitter, unspoken. Anger at life, at himself, perhaps even at God, though he dared not form the thought.

The sanctuary lamp flickered, its red glow spilling across the shadows, a reminder of the Presence that should have been his comfort. But all Mateo felt was the crushing weight of a life marked by wounds too heavy to bear.

And so he knelt there, trembling under the glow of that light, a young man torn between faith and despair, between the call he longed to follow and the shadows that bound him still.

The silence was absolute. The sorrow, unending.

Whispers of Hope and Redemption

The mountain air at dawn carried its usual crisp stillness, the kind of silence that wrapped itself around the retreat house and drew men into contemplation. For most of the novices, the rhythm of prayer, meditation, and silence was slowly shaping them, carving out a quiet joy that gave strength to endure the intensity of the thirty days.

But with Mateo, it was different.

At meals, the others noticed how he hardly touched his food, pushing rice around his plate until the bell ended the silence. During spiritual conferences, his eyes wandered, his hands tightening as though holding back something no one could see. At night, when the retreat house was supposed to rest in the deep quiet of prayer, the novices in the dormitory whispered that Mateo often turned in his bed, sighing, restless, and unable to sleep.

Some pitied him. Others were quietly afraid, for they knew that prolonged unrest could break a man's vocation before it even began.

It was not long before Fr. Carlos, the Assistant Novice Master, observed what the others could only whisper about. Unlike Fr. Ignacio, whose authority weighed heavy in every word, Fr. Carlos carried a softer presence—gentler, but no less piercing. He had a way of looking at a novice as though seeing beneath the silence to the turmoil within.

One late afternoon, as the bell for spiritual reading faded into the mountain air, Fr. Carlos approached Mateo by the cloister walk. The young man stood alone, staring at the fading sun, lips pressed tight as if holding back a cry.

"Mateo," Fr. Carlos began, his voice low, almost fatherly. "I've noticed how heavy these days have been for you. This retreat is meant to purify, yes—but not to crush."

Mateo turned slowly, avoiding his gaze.

Fr. Carlos stepped closer, lowering his tone. "Tell me, son… is there something you carry that makes this silence unbearable? Do you still desire this path—the priesthood—or is it slipping away from you?"

The words sank deep, almost too direct. Mateo's heart pounded. He wanted to answer, yet the fear of exposure kept him mute.

But the gentleness in Fr. Carlos' eyes was unrelenting. "You don't have to walk this alone," he added softly. "If you need help, if you need guidance, I am here. But you must be honest—with yourself and with God."

Mateo swallowed hard, his silence betraying both resistance and desperation. The choice loomed before him: to open his wounds once more or to retreat further into himself.

The mountains grew darker, the first stars pressing through the sky, as if heaven itself leaned close to hear what Mateo would say.

Mateo lowered his head, unable to answer the question that Fr. Carlos pressed upon him. His silence was almost suffocating, broken only by the faint hum of crickets waking in the dusk.

Fr. Carlos did not push further at first. He let the quiet stretch, then spoke in a tone that was both gentle and startlingly clear:

"Mateo… not every man who enters a novitiate is called to the priesthood."

Mateo's head lifted slightly, his brow furrowing.

"Some," Fr. Carlos continued, "discover their path is not at the altar, but in a life hidden from the world—silent, prayerful, detached from formation houses and academic life. Some become priests. Others, monks."

Mateo's eyes widened, the words striking him like a sudden wind in the stillness.

Fr. Carlos allowed the thought to settle before continuing. "There is a monastery, far from here—on another island. The Trappist Monastery. Their life is different. Every hour of the day is shaped by pure silence, strict discipline, and a rhythm of prayer. No choir of seminarians, no parish expectations. Just God, and the soul laid bare before Him."

Mateo felt something stir within—fear and relief mingled together. "Monks," he whispered, as though tasting the word for the first time.

"Yes," Fr. Carlos said with a small, knowing nod. "The Trappists. They do not preach in the streets or teach in the schools. Their mission is hidden, yet powerful. A man who cannot bear the noise of the world may still find God in the silence of the cloister."

"But… how?" Mateo asked, his voice breaking, almost childlike. "How could I even begin something like that?"

Fr. Carlos' face softened. "You will not be alone. If your heart truly longs for such a path, I will help you. I know their Abbot. I can speak with him on your behalf. The process of transferring will take time—letters, permissions, a period of discernment—but it is possible. And I will guide you every step."

Mateo's chest tightened. For the first time in weeks, he felt the faintest glimmer of something apart from despair. The idea of silence, of a life where no one demanded answers from him, where his past might dissolve into the rhythm of prayer and work—it was both terrifying and strangely liberating.

His eyes brimmed, not with peace, but with the shock of possibility. He looked at Fr. Carlos, almost clinging to his presence. "And… you would really help me?"

Fr. Carlos placed a firm hand on his shoulder. "All the way, Mateo. Whatever God is asking of you, I will walk with you until you can see it clearly."

The sanctuary lamp flickered in the distance, casting its light over the cloister. Mateo stood trembling—not in fear this time, but in the uneasy awakening of a choice he never imagined.

CHAPTER 13

An Alternative Path

The days of the retreat had worn Mateo thin, like a candle burning too fast and too unevenly, wax dripping in restless shapes. He rose with the others for prayer and sat in the chapel through the prescribed meditations, but his heart remained elsewhere, restless, untethered. The silence of the retreat, which was meant to lead souls to God, felt to him like a heavy fog through which no voice could be heard clearly—not even the voice of heaven.

It was in the quiet of an afternoon walk, when the shadows of the pine trees stretched long across the mountain path, that Fr. Carlos drew close once more. Mateo's gait was sluggish, his eyes tired, but Fr. Carlos spoke with a firm gentleness.

"Mateo," he began, "I have been thinking about what we discussed. About the Trappist Monastery."

Mateo swallowed, his pulse quickening. The thought had haunted him since their first conversation—haunted, yet strangely consoled.

Fr. Carlos paused, looking at him intently. "I believe it is not wise to let this linger. You are unraveling in this retreat; I can see it every day. To force you through the remaining days might only deepen your unrest. Perhaps... it would be better if we returned to Santa Monica now. There, we can make the arrangements. Letters, permissions, introductions. If this path is truly where God is leading you, there is no point in prolonging your suffering here."

The words hung in the cool mountain air, and for a moment Mateo could not breathe. To leave the retreat early was unthinkable; the thirty-day silence was considered the pinnacle of the novitiate formation, the final proving ground. But to stay felt unbearable. Every chapel hour was a battlefield, every night a torture of sleeplessness. The voices of his past—the laughter of classmates at San Agustin, the harsh reprimand of Fr. Alvarez, the whisper of Miss Lolita's shadow—all pressed harder against him in the stillness.

And yet, here was Fr. Carlos, not condemning his weakness but opening a door.

"Leave… now?" Mateo asked, his voice barely steady.

"Yes," Fr. Carlos said firmly. "There is no shame in it. Some journeys take different turns. What matters is that you do not hide from where God may be truly calling you. We will speak to Fr. Ignacio, of course, but I will stand with you in this."

Mateo felt something inside him tremble—not the tremor of fear, but of relief. A way out. A path he had never imagined: the cloistered life of the Trappists, hidden on an island far from the judging eyes of seminary halls. He imagined their silence not as a weight but as a refuge, where he could bury his sorrows in prayer and routine, where no one would press him to reveal wounds he could barely understand himself.

That night, as the other novices filed into the chapel for yet another hour of silent prayer, Mateo lingered near the doorway. His gaze fell on the sanctuary lamp, burning steadily above the tabernacle. For days it had mocked him with its unwavering flame. Tonight, however, it seemed to flicker—not with accusation, but with possibility.

He sank into a pew, his body weary, his heart aching. He whispered a prayer that was less a plea and more a surrender: If this is the path You want for me, Lord… let me walk it.

And as the chapel filled with the muted sound of shifting robes and whispered breaths, Mateo clung to the single thread of hope Fr. Carlos had handed him: that perhaps his story did not have to end in failure but in a different kind of beginning—far away, in the silence of a contemplative life in a monastery.

CHAPTER 14

A Sense of Disappointment

The news spread quietly, but among novices silence could not bury the weight of such a decision. When Fr. Ignacio gathered them that morning in the chapel, his face was composed, but his eyes betrayed unease. Mateo sat in the back, his head lowered, feeling every gaze upon him even before words were spoken.

"Brothers," Fr. Ignacio began, "one of our number will be leaving the retreat earlier than planned. He has discerned, with counsel, that the Lord may be leading him along a different path. His departure is not failure—this is fidelity to God's voice, however mysterious it may sound."

No name was mentioned, but everyone knew. Mateo's chest burned as though the sanctuary lamp itself were searing him. Some of the novices stole quick glances in his direction; others fixed their eyes stubbornly on their prayer books, unwilling to betray curiosity or judgment. The silence was heavier than any words.

Later that morning, in the small office where stacks of spiritual reading lined the shelves, Mateo faced Fr. Ignacio. The Novice Master's tone was measured, but Mateo felt the weight behind it.

"You will not finish the thirty days, Mateo," Fr. Ignacio said slowly, almost sorrowfully. "This is highly irregular. The Ignatian retreat is meant to strip you bare, to reveal what lies beneath your soul. And what lies beneath you, I fear, is unrest that has not yet found its root."

Mateo bit his lip. He wanted to protest, to defend himself, to say that the silence was not helping him but destroying him. Yet he could not form the words. Instead, he bowed his head, his fingers trembling on his knees.

It was Fr. Carlos who spoke. "Father, I have counseled Mateo. Perhaps his path is not ours. The monastery offers a different way of life, equally consecrated, equally faithful. Some are called to shepherd; others are called to pray in silence for the world. We must not bind God's hand by insisting on only one mold."

Fr. Ignacio's eyes narrowed. His silence stretched so long that Mateo thought the air itself would break. Finally, with a sigh, he nodded. "If this is truly where he believes the Lord is leading him, then I will not stand in the way. But, Mateo—" his voice deepened, carrying a note of warning—"know that the monastery is not an escape. It is a crucible. You cannot outrun what haunts you; you can only face it before God."

The words pierced Mateo, but he dared not respond.

Two days later, with the retreat still unfinished, Mateo packed his few belongings. The other novices watched him quietly as he placed his breviary and rosary into a small bag. None spoke, though their eyes said much—pity, confusion, even relief that it was not they who were leaving.

When he stepped out of the retreat house, the mountain air felt both fresh and heavy. Fr. Carlos walked beside him, his presence steady, almost fatherly. Together they began the descent down the stone path that wound toward the waiting transportation that would carry them back to Santa Monica.

At the last turn of the path, Mateo glanced back at the retreat house, its white walls gleaming in the sun. It stood like a fortress he had failed to conquer, a place that would forever hold part of his story. His chest ached with sorrow and shame, yet somewhere deep within, beneath the trembling, a sliver of hope glimmered: perhaps, beyond the sea, behind monastery walls, he might finally find peace.

And so he walked on, the sound of gravel crunching beneath his sandals, carrying with him the weight of his past—and the fragile promise of another beginning.

Chapter 15

Unfinished Retreat?

The car rumbled into the familiar courtyard of Santa Monica Seminary, its engine coughing dust into the afternoon air. Mateo felt his stomach twist as he stepped down, clutching his small bag. It was as though the walls themselves were whispering about him, old stone witnesses to his return. He had left this place once before with certainty in his heart; now he returned carrying a silence that weighed more than words.

Inside, the corridors buzzed with the muted life of seminarians in study and recreation. Yet the moment Mateo entered, conversations stilled. A few glanced at him, then quickly looked away. Others exchanged subtle nods, lips pressed into knowing lines. Rumors traveled swiftly in a house of men devoted to prayer but still very human in curiosity.

"Did you hear?" one whispered in the corner of the refectory.

"They say he couldn't finish the thirty-day retreat."

"Fr. Ignacio sent him home."

"No… I heard it was his choice."

"Either way, it means something broke."

The words, half-truths strung into judgments, followed Mateo like shadows. He ate in silence, pushing rice across his plate, his ears burning. No one spoke to him directly, yet he felt exposed, as if his failure were written plainly on his forehead.

That evening, in the rector's office, Fr. Carlos sat with Mateo across from the heavy mahogany desk. Papers rustled as Fr. Carlos laid out his intention clearly.

"Mateo, I will speak with the Abbot of the Trappist Monastery. It may take some time, but I believe they will accept you. Their life is different—harsher, simpler, quieter. But perhaps this is what your soul needs."

Mateo's lips quivered before he could form words. "Father… what if they reject me too?"

Fr. Carlos leaned forward, his eyes kind yet steady. "Rejection does not come from God, Mateo. It comes from fear—ours or others'. If God wills this path, He will open the doors. If He does not, then you must believe He is leading you somewhere even you cannot yet see."

Mateo nodded, though the tremor in his hands betrayed him.

Days passed in waiting. He walked the seminary grounds, avoiding long gazes, hiding in the library with books he could not focus on, and sitting by the chapel door rather than inside, as though afraid to step fully into prayer. The sanctuary lamp flickered, and with it came memories—Santa Ana's shadows, San Agustin's corridors, Fr. Alvarez's piercing stare, and now Fr. Ignacio's troubling words. They blended into one unbroken chorus: You are not fit. You will not last.

One night, unable to sleep, Mateo slipped into the chapel. Kneeling before the altar, he pressed his forehead to the cold marble step. "Lord," he whispered through clenched teeth, "if the priesthood is not mine, and if silence in the monastery is what You ask, then take me there. But if this life too ends in sorrow… if I am to be cast away again… then why did You call me at all?"

The darkness gave no answer. Only the sanctuary lamp burned above him, its glow steady, unyielding.

CHAPTER 16

A Period of Observership

The letter arrived on a gray afternoon, carried by the seminary porter, who slipped it quietly into Fr. Carlos' hands. The envelope bore no grand seal, only the simple handwriting of the Trappist Abbot. The simplicity itself felt like a sign—no need for embellishment, only truth.

Fr. Carlos called Mateo into his office. The young novice entered slowly, as if bracing himself for another wound. His eyes darted to the envelope on the desk, then back to Fr. Carlos' face.

"It is from the Monastery," Fr. Carlos said gently. "Sit, Mateo."

With careful deliberation, he opened the letter and read aloud.

"The Abbot of Our Lady of the Desert greets you in Christ. After prayer and discernment, we are willing to receive Mateo Aragon for a period of observership within our community. This time shall not yet make him a monk, but it will allow him to experience our life of silence, labor, and prayer. The period shall last six months, during which he must obey our Rule entirely. At the end, the community shall discern together with him if he is truly called to remain."

Fr. Carlos lowered the paper and looked at Mateo. "They are opening the door, but with strict conditions. You will be watched, Mateo. Not with suspicion, but with clarity. They will want to see if you can carry silence, if you can bear the solitude without it breaking you."

Mateo's lips parted, but no sound came out. His chest heaved as if a great stone pressed upon him. At last he whispered, "Six months… what will happen if I fail again?"

Fr. Carlos leaned forward, his voice steady. "Then you will have tried. And in the trying, God will reveal something to you—perhaps more than you seek now. Mateo, the worst thing is not to fail. The worst thing is never to step where grace is calling."

Tears blurred Mateo's sight. He pressed his palms together, trembling. Grace calling… or exile again? The two were indistinguishable in his heart. Yet beneath the sorrow, something flickered—a possibility, a path that was neither rejection nor the priesthood as he once dreamed, but something else, something harder and hidden.

That evening, as the bell rang for Vespers, Mateo remained in the chapel after the others had gone. He stared at the crucifix, Christ suspended between heaven and earth, abandoned yet surrendered. "If You could endure Your silence, Lord," Mateo murmured, "perhaps I can endure mine."

The sanctuary lamp glowed faintly above him. For the first time in weeks, its flame did not accuse but beckoned.

CHAPTER 17

Silence Will Teach You

The morning Mateo left Santa Monica, the sky hung low with mist. The novices stood in silence as he gathered his few belongings—no one dared speak, though their eyes followed him with a mixture of pity and curiosity. Whispers had already spread: Mateo was leaving before the retreat had ended, leaving before vows, leaving for something none of them understood.

Fr. Carlos accompanied him to the port. Their steps echoed against the cobbled path, the mountains behind them slowly disappearing into the haze. Neither spoke much; words had become too fragile. But just before they boarded the ferry, Fr. Carlos turned to Mateo.

"Remember," he said, "this is not a flight from pain. It must be a walk toward God. If you treat it only as an escape, the silence will crush you. But if you let it be a gift, the silence will teach you."

Mateo nodded, clutching his worn satchel. His heart pounded as the boat pulled away from shore, the seminary walls shrinking into the distance like a dream dissolving at dawn. The salt air filled his lungs, and for the first time, he felt the vastness of his choice—he was heading toward a life unknown, perhaps forever unseen by the world.

Hours later, the island appeared on the horizon, green and wild, untouched by the noise of cities. The Trappist Monastery rose like a hidden fortress among trees, its stone walls simple, unadorned, yet unyielding. A bell tower reached skyward, but no sound broke from it, as though even the bell had sworn silence.

Two monks met Mateo at the gate. Their faces were calm, unreadable. Without a word, one gestured for him to follow. They led him through a cloister garden where the only sound was the rustle of leaves. Everything about the place felt stripped bare—no decorations, no excess, only prayer woven into stone.

At the chapter room, the Abbot awaited. He was an elderly man with eyes as sharp as winter stars yet softened by years of contemplation.

"Welcome, Mateo," he said simply. "You shall stay among us for six months. You will keep silence, rise when the bell calls, labor in the fields, and pray the hours. In silence, we discover if God has written your name among us."

Mateo bowed his head, overwhelmed. "Yes, Father."

That night, he lay on a thin mattress in his cell, a crucifix on the wall above him, the wind rattling faintly against the shutters. There were no voices, no music, and no laughter from novices. Only silence—thick, vast, pressing upon him like a second skin.

And yet, as he closed his eyes, the words of Fr. Carlos echoed in his heart: If you let it be a gift, the silence will teach you.

The lamp flickered, and Mateo prayed with all the fragility of his soul: "Lord, do not abandon me here. If this is where You want me, give me the strength to stay."

CHAPTER 18

Who Are You, Mateo?

The bell tolled at three o'clock in the morning. A sound sharp and heavy, echoing through the monastery like a hammer against the silence. Mateo woke with a start, disoriented, his breath clouding faintly in the chill of the stone cell. He had only just fallen asleep—or so it seemed. The thin blanket clung to him with little warmth. Still, he rose.

The corridor outside was dim, lit only by a lantern at the far end. Other monks, shadows in their white cowls, moved quietly toward the chapel. No words were spoken. Their sandals whispered against the stone floor, every step measured and deliberate.

In the chapel, the air was thick with the scent of wax and ancient wood. The monks gathered in two rows facing each other, voices breaking the silence with the chanting of Matins. A low, resonant hum filled the space, carrying words Mateo barely understood, yet felt deep within him. He stumbled over the Latin verses, his voice faint and uncertain, but no one turned to correct him.

When the last note faded, silence returned—denser, heavier than before. Mateo felt it press against him, as if the walls themselves demanded his surrender.

After prayer came labor. The Abbot assigned Mateo to the fields. The soil was damp from the night's mist, and the work was backbreaking. He dug, carried, and planted under the pale light of dawn. Around him, the monks labored with quiet focus, no complaints, no chatter. The only sound was the rhythm of tools striking the earth. Mateo's muscles ached, his hands blistered, but he kept at it, unwilling to falter in front of men who seemed carved from patience itself.

By midday, they gathered for their frugal meal: bread, vegetables, and water. They ate in silence while one monk read aloud from Scripture. Mateo chewed slowly, his stomach unsatisfied, his heart restless. He longed for conversation, for a voice to break the stillness. But all he heard was the steady reading and the scrape of wooden spoons.

Days turned into a rhythm: prayer, work, silence. Rising before dawn, laboring until dusk, kneeling until his knees throbbed, walking in gardens where the only sound was birdsong. At first, it was suffocating. Mateo's thoughts crowded in, memories of San Agustin, the Diocesan Seminary, Santa Monica, and especially of Miss Lolita. Her face haunted him like an unwelcome guest. He tried to push her image away, yet the silence only sharpened it, as though God was forcing him to confront what he had buried.

At night, he trembled in his cell. The silence became a mirror, and what stared back was his brokenness—his confusion, his unworthiness, and his gnawing doubts about vocation. He sometimes pressed his palms against his ears, desperate for noise, for anything to drown out the roar of his own thoughts.

And yet—slowly, almost imperceptibly—something began to shift.

One morning, as he tilled the soil, Mateo lifted his eyes and saw the sunrise spread across the horizon. The sky blazed with gold and crimson, spilling light upon the monastery walls. In that moment, for the first time, he felt no ache of restlessness, no weight of shame. Only a quiet stirring, like a whisper in his soul: Here I am. Here you are. That is enough.

Another evening, kneeling in the chapel, the chanting of the monks rose around him like waves. Mateo's voice joined, tentative at first, then stronger. The rhythm of prayer seemed to stitch his fractured heart back together. For the first time in years, he did not feel entirely lost.

But the silence was not only a gift; it was also a trial. By the second week, Mateo's resolve began to waver. The memories returned with greater force—Fr. Alvarez's warning, Fr. Ignacio's probing eyes, and the voice that told him he was unfit. In the stillness of night, he almost believed them. He wondered if the Trappists, too, would one day discover what he carried and cast him out as well.

He fought with himself daily: was this truly God's will, or only another failed attempt at belonging?

The Abbot noticed his turmoil. One afternoon, after Vespers, he called Mateo to the cloister garden. The Abbot's gaze was piercing but not unkind. "Silence is like a mirror, son," he said. "It will not hide you. It will show you who you are. Most men flee from that reflection. Few endure it. If you remain, the mirror will also show you who God is. But you must not be afraid of what it shows you first."

Mateo bowed his head, shaken by the words. He wanted to believe he could endure, but the shadows of his past loomed large.

That night, lying in the narrow cell, he whispered a prayer he had never dared to speak before: "Lord… if I am not meant to be a priest, or even a monk, then let me not waste my life. Show me who I am, even if it hurts."

The crucifix above his bed seemed to glow faintly in the candlelight, silent but present. Mateo closed his eyes, uncertain of what tomorrow would bring.

The bell would ring again at three. And the silence would ask him again: Who are you, Mateo Aragon?

CHAPTER 19

Lectio Divina

The bell rang again at three in the morning. By now, Mateo no longer woke startled. His body, though weary, had begun to accept the rhythm of the monastery. Still, every time he rose from the thin mat, he felt the same tightening in his chest—the same sense that each day was a trial he was barely enduring.

The chapel was cold, its stone walls breathing with dampness. The monks took their places, white habits rustling softly in the darkness. When the chanting began, Mateo allowed the words to pass over him like a tide. He still stumbled on the Latin, but he no longer tried to keep up perfectly. Instead, he let the melody draw him into the silence between words.

It was in those pauses—when no sound filled the air—that Mateo's heart beat loudest.

After the prayers, they filed silently into the cloister walk. The monastery was still wrapped in shadow, the air heavy with mist from the sea. Mateo noticed the details he had once overlooked: the dew on the grass, the hush of waves against distant rocks, and the faint scent of jasmine clinging to the air. In silence, the world spoke.

Work filled the hours after dawn. The Abbot had assigned him to the gardens, where rows of vegetables grew with disciplined order. Mateo worked with another novice, a young man named Brother Samuel, who had been at the monastery for almost a year. Samuel rarely spoke, even during the short times when silence was permitted, but his gestures were patient and kind. He showed Mateo how to tend the seedlings with care, how to prune without wounding, and how to dig without damaging the roots. There was something calming in his presence, as though silence for him was not a burden but a gift. Mateo envied him.

At midday, the community gathered again in the refectory. The same meal: bread, vegetables, and fruit. The same ritual: a monk reading Scripture while the others ate in silence. Mateo chewed slowly, staring at the rough wooden table. The words of Scripture reached his ears, but his mind wandered—always back to his past. To the seminary corridors, to the faces of fellow novices, to the disquieting memory of Miss Lolita's laughter. He bit into his bread harder, trying to drown the thoughts.

The Abbot noticed. That evening, after Vespers, he called Mateo aside.

"You are still restless," he said. His voice was low but carried authority.

Mateo lowered his eyes. "Yes, Father."

"The silence is not your enemy," the Abbot continued. "It only brings forward what you have tried to bury. That is why it feels like a torment. But you must face what rises in you. If you run again, you will meet the same ghosts wherever you go."

Those words followed Mateo into his narrow cell that night. He lay awake, staring at the crucifix. His heart throbbed with unease. What if the Abbot was right? What if his life had become nothing but a flight from one place to another—from San Agustin to the seminary, from the seminary to this monastery? Was he running, or was he searching? He could not tell anymore.

The next day, he was introduced to Lectio Divina, the monks' way of praying with Scripture. One of the older brothers guided him. "Do not read for knowledge," the monk whispered. "Read to listen. Let the Word speak to you."

Mateo opened to the Psalms. His eyes fell on the words: "Be still, and know that I am God." He read it once. Twice. A third time. Each reading pierced him differently. The command "be still" struck his restlessness. The assurance I am God unsettled his doubts. He wanted to believe that stillness was possible, but his mind buzzed like an unquiet hive.

He stayed in the chapel long after the others had left, repeating the verse silently. Be still… be still… He pressed his forehead to the wooden pew, as if the words might carve themselves into his soul. Yet, as silence deepened, another image pushed its way forward: Miss Lolita's eyes, soft but filled with an unspoken longing. He clenched his fists, ashamed that even here, in a place consecrated to silence, his heart betrayed him.

Nights were the hardest. By day, labor gave him something to cling to—tasks that filled his hands and chants that filled his ears. But at night, when the cell swallowed him whole, the silence became a cavern. His doubts returned in a torrent. What if I do not belong here? What if the Abbot is wrong about me? What if God has never called me at all?

He remembered Fr. Carlos, who had sent him here filled with hope. Would he be disappointed if Mateo failed again? And what of the other novices back at the retreat house—did they wonder where he had gone, or had they already forgotten him?

And then, sometimes, another thought crept in, softer but more dangerous: What if I returned to the world altogether? What if I lived as an ordinary man, married, worked, and sought God in the noise of life instead of its silence?

But each time he imagined it, something resisted. It was not pride nor duty, but a fragile spark that whispered, "Stay." "Endure." "Wait."

On the fifteenth day of his stay, the Abbot summoned him to his office. The room was bare except for a crucifix and a single wooden desk. The Abbot's eyes studied Mateo carefully.
"Do you wish to continue?" he asked.

Mateo hesitated. He wanted to say yes. He wanted to say no. Instead, his voice broke: "I don't know."

The Abbot nodded, untroubled by his indecision. "That is a good answer," he said. "Those who are too certain at the beginning often do not last. It is better to say, 'I don't know,' and wait for God to teach you. Here, knowing is less important than enduring. If you endure, the truth will come."

Mateo left the room shaken but strangely comforted. For the first time, he realized he did not have to declare himself yet. He only had to remain. He needed to endure the silence and his own heart.

That night, as he knelt in his cell, the verse returned: "Be still, and know that I am God." He repeated it until his breathing slowed, until his racing thoughts loosened their grip. For the briefest moment, the silence did not accuse him—it embraced him.

The bell would ring again at three. Tomorrow would come with its trials. But tonight, Mateo surrendered to the stillness, whispering the only prayer he could manage:

"Lord, let me stay long enough to find out who I am."

CHAPTER 20

The Accident in the Fields

The bell rang early that morning, cutting through the misty silence of the monastery grounds. The Abbot had announced during Vigils that the day's work would not be the usual tending of gardens or maintenance of the monastery's orchards. Instead, everyone would head to the sloping hills behind the cloister to cut firebreaks—wide, clear paths in the thick grass and scrub to prevent the spread of bushfires. It was hard, grueling labor, but necessary.

The monks moved with quiet determination, sickles in hand, their brown robes tucked at the waist to allow freer movement. The sound of steel slicing through brush filled the air, mingling with the distant cries of birds startled from their nests. The sun had barely risen, but sweat already glistened on their foreheads.

Mateo worked alongside them, awkward at first with the sickle but eager to do his share. Each swing of the blade seemed to him both a prayer and a trial—proof that he was willing to humble himself, to learn a different rhythm of life. He thought briefly of the music he once made, of choirs and carols, and how far from those moments he now stood. Here, there was no audience, no applause—only the silent witness of the earth and sky.

Then it happened.

As Mateo bent to cut through a particularly stubborn clump of grass, his hand slipped. The sickle's edge caught his left little finger, slicing deep before he could pull back. A sharp sting exploded through him, followed by a warm rush of blood. His hand recoiled instinctively, the sickle falling into the grass.

"Brother!" Mateo cried, his voice breaking the steady silence. One of the nearby monks, Brother Thomas, dropped his work and rushed to him. Seeing the blood flowing, Thomas quickly tore a strip of cloth from his sleeve, wrapping it tightly around Mateo's finger. "Come—we must go to the infirmary."

They half-ran, half-walked down the narrow path to the monastery's small infirmary. The smell of herbs and antiseptic filled the room as another monk, the Infirmarian, prepared bandages. Mateo's face was pale, his lips pressed together, but his eyes betrayed both pain and fear.

Trying to break the heaviness of the moment, Mateo gave a shaky laugh. "Tell me the truth, Brother… Am I going to lose my little finger? Because if I do, I might as well die."

The Infirmarian looked up, surprised.

Mateo continued, almost desperately, "You see… without this finger, I can no longer play the guitar… or the piano. And if I can't play… then what am I, Brother? What will I be?"

Brother Thomas chuckled softly, shaking his head. "You won't lose your finger, Mateo. The cut is deep, yes, but it will heal. It may take some time before you can play again—but your finger will be back in its place. God gave you music, Mateo. He will not take it from you so easily."

The reassurance struck Mateo like a balm. Relief flooded his chest, and his eyes brimmed with tears. For the first time since he entered the monastery, he realized how deeply he feared losing the one gift that had anchored him since childhood. His voice, his music, his fingers—these were more than talents; they were his way of existing in the world.

The bandaging finished, Mateo was told to rest. Work in the fields was no longer possible for him. The accident meant that his stay in the monastery, originally intended for six months, would now be prolonged. Healing required time, and time was something the monastery gave abundantly.

Later that night, as Mateo lay on his cot with his hand carefully wrapped, he reflected on the strange twist of fate. What if the accident had been worse? What if his finger truly had been lost? The thought shook him. He realized then that his calling—whether priest, monk, or something else entirely—could never be separated from the music that pulsed through him. Music was his breath, his prayer, his lifeline.

The monastery was teaching him silence, but God had carved into him a song.

And now, forced to remain longer within these walls of prayer and labor, Mateo wondered if perhaps this was God's way of keeping him still—long enough to listen, long enough to discover what was truly asked of him.

The days passed slowly after the accident. Mateo's finger, bound in clean white cloth, throbbed with each heartbeat, a constant reminder of his vulnerability. The work in the fields continued without him, and he often watched from the cloister windows as the other monks moved like shadows in the sun, cutting and clearing with steady rhythm.

At first, he felt restless. To be still while others worked weighed on him like guilt. But the Abbot, seeing his unease, spoke gently one evening after Compline:

"Do not mistake rest for uselessness, Brother Mateo. There are many ways to labor in the monastery. Some work with hands, others with heart. Perhaps your task now is to listen to what God wishes to say in your stillness."

Those words stayed with him.

Confined to the infirmary's quiet corner, Mateo began humming to himself to pass the time. At first, they were aimless melodies, drifting like smoke. But soon, one tune returned—faint, persistent, like an echo from another life. He remembered it clearly then: the first melody he had ever truly written, back when he was just a freshman at San Agustin High School.

Back then, Literature class had felt overwhelming. The oral exams required them to memorize long, ornate poems. Mateo, struggling with the lines, had taken to setting the words to music—simple progressions on his guitar, weaving rhythm into memory. That was how he first discovered the power of music, not just as art, but as survival.

Now, in the monastery's stillness, the old progression returned to him. The rise and fall of it was simple, almost childlike, yet there was a beauty in its purity. He closed his eyes, mouthing the words of the poem he once used to memorize. But they no longer fit. They belonged to a younger Mateo, a boy just beginning to find his voice.

Instead, new words came—hesitant at first, then flowing like water breaking through a stone. He whispered them into the silence, testing their shape against the melody.

Longing to be what I am,
not what others see or demand.
A voice within still calls my name.
through silence, through fire, through pain.

He paused, his throat tightening. These were not the words of a high school boy trying to pass an exam. These were the words of a man wrestling with himself, searching for a truth he could finally claim.

Night after night, he returned to the song, refining each phrase, shifting lines until they carried the weight of his longing. He titled it *Longing To Be What I Am*. The name itself felt like both a confession and a prayer.

One evening, Brother Thomas found him sitting by the infirmary window, humming softly as his bandaged hand tapped an invisible guitar.

"You've been singing more these days," Thomas observed.

Mateo smiled sheepishly. "It's an old song… or maybe a new one. I don't know anymore. I wrote it first when I was in high school. I changed it now. It feels like it belongs to me in a way it didn't before."

Thomas nodded. "Perhaps God gave it back to you for this very reason. To remind you that your gift is not only for yourself but for Him."

Mateo's eyes grew moist. He realized then that the accident, painful as it was, had slowed him long enough to rediscover something essential. Music was not merely his skill—it was the truest way he prayed.

As the monastery bells tolled across the night, Mateo whispered the refrain once more, each word a seed planted in the silence:

Longing to be what I am…
Lord, let me be what I am…

And in that quiet, Mateo felt for the first time that perhaps his path was not about choosing between priesthood or monkhood, but about becoming fully himself—whoever God intended him to be.

Chapter 21

Days at the Infirmary

The infirmary days stretched into weeks, and Mateo's little finger, though tender, slowly regained its strength. By the time he could bend it again without flinching, the monastery had entered a new rhythm: the planting season had passed, and now came the quieter tasks of upkeep and preparation for the next cycle.

But for Mateo, the turning point came one afternoon when the Prior entered the refectory at midday with a simple announcement.

"Brother Rafael might return to his family for some weeks," he said, his voice steady yet tinged with concern. "His mother's health requires his presence. We shall pray for her recovery. In the meantime, we will need someone to take his place at the organ for the Divine Office when he's gone."

A soft murmur spread across the tables. Brother Rafael had been the organist for decades. His playing was not showy, but it anchored the community's chanting with a quiet stability. To imagine the hours of Lauds, Vespers, and Compline without his guiding chords felt almost unthinkable.

The Prior scanned the room and, as if directed by an unseen force, focused his gaze on Mateo.

"Brother Mateo, perhaps you can serve us in this role for now. I have heard you are no stranger to music."

Mateo froze, the spoon in his hand hovering over his bowl. His first instinct was to protest. He was still an outsider, barely acclimated to monastic life, uncertain of his own path. To be entrusted with something so integral to the monastery's daily rhythm seemed far beyond him.

Yet all eyes had turned to him, some curious, others quietly supportive. He nodded, his throat dry. "Yes, Father Prior. I will do my best."

That evening, Mateo sat alone in the chapel, the faint smell of incense still clinging to the air. The organ loomed before him—larger, older, and far more intricate than the upright piano of his childhood or the guitars of his youth. He touched the worn keys tentatively, their coolness sending a shiver through him.

At first, he stumbled. The timing of the chants was different from the pieces he once knew, and the mechanics of the organ demanded more than just dexterity—it demanded listening and breathing with the community.

But gradually, as he played through the psalm tones and simple hymns, a calm washed over him. The monks' voices, steady and resonant, filled the chapel. His task was not to perform but to support them, to give them a foundation. The organ was not for him—it was for them, for God.

Later that week, after Compline, Mateo lingered at the bench. The chapel was empty, lit only by the flicker of sanctuary lamps. His fingers, almost instinctively, drifted into the melody he had been nursing in the infirmary—*Longing To Be What I Am.*

The notes spilled softly across the stone walls, weaving between silence and shadow. He sang only a fragment, his voice low, almost a whisper.

> *Longing to be what I am,*
> *not what others see or demand…*

He didn't notice Brother Thomas had entered until he heard a bench creak nearby. Startled, Mateo turned, but Thomas only smiled, eyes glimmering in the dim light.

"Don't stop," Thomas said gently. "That song belongs here."

Mateo's chest tightened. Something within him stirred—an almost terrifying thought. Could it be that his music, the gift he once feared might hold no place in a monastery, was in fact the very reason he had been led here?

The next day, as the monks chanted Lauds with Mateo accompanying, there was a new steadiness in him. His hands, though still healing, moved with quiet confidence. The organ's notes carried not only the weight of tradition but also the tender hope of a man discovering that perhaps God had not asked him to give up his gift—only to give it back, in a different form.

CHAPTER 22

A Break from the Silence

Life in the Trappist Monastery followed a rhythm that was as steady as breath—work, prayer, silence, and rest. But even within such order, there was room for the human spirit to find gentle release. Sundays, after Vespers, carried a different atmosphere.

It was the one time in the week when the Great Silence was relaxed for a while. The monks gathered in the cloister garden or in the common room, where voices replaced the hum of tools and laughter punctuated the solemnity of their usual days. Stories were exchanged, often humorous, sometimes profound, each one a glimpse into the lives they had left behind or the grace they had found within these walls.

On one such Sunday, Mateo found himself sitting among them, his guitar resting on his lap. Brother Thomas had encouraged him to bring it along.

"Play something," Thomas urged, smiling.

Mateo hesitated at first, glancing around at the circle of brown-robed figures. These were men who had renounced the world, men of silence—would they truly care for his song? Still, something in their expectant gazes gave him courage.

He began softly, his fingers coaxing out a simple progression, a melody he had carried since his high school days but reshaped now, matured by years of searching. Then, in the dimming light of Sunday evening, he sang:

"Longing To Be What I Am"

When the final chord faded, silence followed—not the awkward kind, but the silence that held reverence. A few brothers had their eyes closed, lips moving silently as if in prayer. Others simply watched Mateo with a quiet smile.

Brother Anselm broke the stillness with a chuckle. "So we have a troubadour among us," he said warmly. "Careful, Mateo, or you'll turn us into singers instead of monks."

The circle erupted in gentle laughter, light and sincere. Mateo blushed but felt something stir in his heart. For the first time since he had entered the monastery, he felt that his gift had not been left behind—it had found a home. His music was no longer for applause but for communion, for brotherhood.

And as the brothers went on sharing stories and laughter late into the evening, Mateo realized that his song had not merely been entertainment. It had become a mirror of their shared journey: leaving behind the world, facing tribulations, yet finding in God a place where they could truly be themselves.

CHAPTER 23

The Appointed Organist

The old organ in the chapel had stood for decades, its pipes weathered yet still capable of filling the vaulted stone space with sound both majestic and tender. For as long as Mateo had been at the monastery, it was Brother Rafael who sat faithfully at the bench during Lauds, Vespers, and Mass, his hands steady, his timing impeccable.

But one morning, after Prime, the Abbot gathered the brothers in the cloister and announced, "It's time for Brother Rafael to go home to his family for a few weeks. His family urgently requires his presence, and we have given him our blessing to go."

There was a murmur of assent, a small ripple of sympathy among the monks. Family ties, though often loosened in monastic life, were never denied. Rafael bowed and received their silent prayers.

Then the Abbot's gaze turned toward Mateo. "Brother Mateo, you will serve as organist until Rafael returns."

The words startled him. He had expected many duties—fieldwork, cleaning, kitchen labor—but this? This was different. His heart leapt, both in joy and fear.

"Yes, Father Abbot," Mateo replied softly, lowering his head.

The first time he sat at the organ, Mateo trembled. His injured little finger, though healing, was still tender. He flexed it cautiously as he placed his hands on the keys. The brothers began to file into the chapel for Vespers, their footsteps echoing in the hushed space. Mateo's chest tightened.

He closed his eyes for a moment and prayed silently: "Lord, let these hands be Yours. Let this music lift hearts to You."

The Abbot gave the signal. Mateo pressed the first chord.

The sound rose—deep, resonant, alive. The vibrations filled the chapel's stone walls, soaring upward like wings. The monks' chant followed, weaving into the organ's sustained tones a harmony ancient and unbroken.

As he played, Mateo felt something strange and beautiful. It was not performance. There was no audience to impress, no applause waiting at the end. His role was simple but profound: to support the prayer of the community, to let music become a vessel of praise.

His little finger faltered once, missing a note, but the chant carried on undisturbed. Mateo smiled to himself. Perfection was not required—only faithfulness.

After the service, Brother Thomas approached him at the cloister walk. "You play not just with your hands," Thomas said, "but with your heart. That is what the Lord desires."

Mateo nodded, his eyes moist. He remembered his younger years—concert halls, competitions, recitals—when music had been his ambition, his way of proving himself to the world. But here, in the quiet of the monastery, he discovered its truest purpose.

That evening, when the brothers shared their customary Sunday leisure, a few of them teased Mateo kindly. "Our chapel suddenly sounds like Rome itself," joked Brother Anselm. "Careful, or pilgrims might start arriving from nowhere."

Laughter rang again, soft but full. Mateo laughed with them, but inside he carried something deeper:

a conviction that God had not asked him to abandon his gift, only to transform it.

Music was no longer about Mateo Aragon. It was about service. About offering. About becoming small so that something greater could shine through.

And in that moment, he knew that the organ's keys, the guitar's strings, even the silence between notes—all of it was now part of his vocation.

CHAPTER 24

The Telegram

Weeks passed, and Mateo grew into his role as the monastery's organist. The brothers quickly adjusted to his presence at the bench, and even the Abbot would linger sometimes in the chapel after prayers, quietly listening to the way Mateo coaxed gentleness from the worn keys.

One evening after Compline, the Abbot stopped him at the cloister gate. His eyes were warm, full of fatherly affection. "Brother Mateo," he said softly, "it brings me joy to see you here. When you arrived, I wondered if the silence would feel heavy upon you, but instead, it seems you have let it shape your soul. The Lord is doing something in you."

Mateo lowered his head, humbled. He had never received such words before—so simple, yet so affirming. The Abbot's approval felt like a blessing deeper than any applause he had ever earned on stage.

Several weeks later, the monastery gathered in the chapter hall. Mateo had been told that this was the day of his evaluation—a quiet but significant step. For months he had been on probation, observed in prayer, in labor, and in humility. Now the Abbot and the council of brothers would give their judgment.

The Abbot rose. His presence carried both solemnity and gentleness. "Brothers, we are here today to decide whether Brother Mateo, who has lived among us in probation, has passed the requirements to begin his novitiate. This is not only about skill or obedience—it is about whether the Lord has indeed planted his vocation here."

Mateo's heart pounded. He folded his trembling hands inside his robe.

But before the Abbot could speak further, the heavy wooden doors opened. Brother Clement entered, slightly breathless, holding a folded paper in his hand. He bowed quickly to the Abbot and whispered, "Forgive the interruption, Father, but this could not wait."

The Abbot paused, accepted the paper, and opened it. His eyes scanned the lines, and his face changed. He folded the telegram carefully, then looked toward Mateo.

"Brother Mateo," the Abbot said, his voice weighted with sorrow, "this is a message from your family. Out of respect, I will not delay in giving it to you."

He stepped forward and placed the telegram in Mateo's shaking hands. The hall was silent.

Mateo's eyes darted across the words. The letters seemed to blur, his breath caught in his throat. Your father has passed away. Come home immediately.

The paper slipped slightly in his grip as his entire body trembled. His lips parted, but no sound came out. He turned to the abbot, his eyes filled with pain, silently asking for guidance, for permission, and for strength.

The Abbot, moved with compassion, placed a hand gently on his shoulder. "Son, I am so sorry. I know this is a wound too sudden for words."

Tears brimmed in Mateo's eyes. "Father Abbot… may I go home? I must…" His voice broke. "…I must see my family."

The Abbot nodded. "Yes, Mateo. Go to them. Family is a sacred gift from God. It would be against charity to keep you here when your mother and kin need you most."

Later, in the Abbot's study, the two sat alone. Mateo still held the telegram in his hand, his knuckles pale from gripping it so tightly.

"Mateo," the Abbot began slowly, "before you leave, I want you to know this: you passed all of our evaluations. Your prayer life, your humility, your obedience—they are real. You have shown us you are ready to live as a monk."

Mateo blinked, stunned. "Then… why…?"

The Abbot's gaze softened with sorrow. "There is only one thing that holds you back. Your age. Our rule requires that a man be twenty-five before he may enter fully. You are nineteen."

The words struck Mateo like another blow. His father was gone. His family needed him. And now, even the life he had begun to love was not yet open to him.

He lowered his head, confusion and anguish twisting inside him. "Why would God let me come this far only to stop me here?"

The Abbot sighed deeply, his eyes glistening with his own unspoken grief. "Perhaps, my son, the Lord is not saying no. Perhaps He is saying not yet. Sometimes, the longest wait serves as His shaping hand.

Mateo said nothing. His body felt heavy, as though the very air pressed down on him. He rose quietly, bowed to the Abbot, and walked back to his cell.

That night, alone in the dim room, he finally let go. He sank to his knees, pressing his face into his hands, and sobbed until his chest ached. Two sorrows had found him in one day: the loss of his father and the postponement of the life he had begun to see as his calling.

The candle on his desk flickered, casting shadows that trembled along the wall. Mateo stared at the telegram again, tears falling onto the ink.

What am I to do now, Lord?

No answer came. Only the sound of his own weeping filled the silence of the cell where hope and despair collided.

CHAPTER 25

Two Heavy Burdens

The monastery bell tolled for Vespers, its sound carrying across the fields and stone cloisters. But Mateo did not join the procession of monks filing silently toward the chapel. Instead, he was seated across from the Abbot in the dimly lit study, his folded telegram resting on the desk like a wound that refused to close.

The Abbot leaned forward, his lined face filled with concern. "My son," he began in a soft voice, "you carry two heavy burdens tonight—the grief of losing your father and the sorrow of your interrupted path here. But God never closes a door without opening another."

Mateo's eyes brimmed, his heart still broken. "Father Abbot, I don't know where to turn. I wanted to stay. I thought perhaps here I had finally found where God wanted me to be." His voice cracked. "Now I must leave. And yet, even if I return, you said my age keeps me away."

The Abbot was silent for a moment, then spoke with words that startled Mateo to his core. "Listen to me, Mateo. I have prayed about you. I believe the Lord's hand is guiding you in a path you may not expect. You must return to San Agustin—continue your studies for the priesthood. If you are called to serve as a priest, you must not resist. The Church needs shepherds as much as it needs monks in silence."

Mateo looked up in shock. He could not believe what he was hearing. "You mean… you are telling me to go back to the seminary? To try again?"

"Yes," the Abbot replied, his eyes firm but tender. "Finish your studies. Discern if God is calling you to the altar. And know this—if after all those years, you still feel drawn to the monastic life, you may return here. I will welcome you back with no questions asked. This will always be your home."

Mateo sat in stunned silence. The very walls of the study seemed to shift around him. He had always trusted Divine Providence—through Santa

Ana, through San Agustin, through the Diocesan Seminary, and now here in this monastery. And yet again, God was reshaping his road, asking him to walk where he did not intend to go.

"Perhaps this is the way, Father Abbot," Mateo whispered, his voice trembling. "Perhaps God is teaching me to trust Him, even when I do not understand."

The Abbot reached across the desk and held his hand firmly. "Yes, Mateo. God shapes us through detours as much as through destinations. Do not lose heart."

The next morning came heavy with silence. Mateo prepared his few belongings without ceremony. The brothers, though unaware of all the details, felt the weight of his departure. They gave him no loud farewells—only gentle embraces, quiet nods, and the silent assurance of their prayers.

For weeks, his guitar had filled their Sunday gatherings with life, and his hands had graced the organ with melodies that lifted weary souls. Now, his absence was already felt. His absence stilled the music that had once filled their cloistered walls.

Mateo walked toward the boat that would take him back to the larger island, each step echoing with uncertainty. He looked once more at the monastery that had become his refuge, then lifted his eyes heavenward.

"Divine Providence," he whispered, "I place myself in Your hands once again."

And with that, he left, carrying his grief, his confusion, and his fragile hope into the unknown.

CHAPTER 26

My Son, You're Home

The small ferry cut through the waters under the gray sky, bringing Mateo back to the larger island. Each wave that slapped against the wooden hull seemed to echo the heaviness of his heart. He carried little with him—just a bundle of clothes, his breviary, and the pain of what he thought was both a personal loss and a broken vocation.

By the time he arrived in San Agustin, evening had begun to fall. The familiar streets welcomed him with the scent of burning firewood and the laughter of children playing in the plaza. Mateo's chest tightened as he walked quickly through the town. His steps led him instinctively to the one place he longed for—home.

When he reached the small gate of their humble house, he paused for a moment, gathering his courage. His heart was torn between grief for his father's death and the anticipation of his mother's embrace. He pushed the gate open and stepped into the small yard.

His mother was just stepping out of the doorway when she saw him. Her eyes widened, and her lips parted in astonishment. Then, in an instant, she ran forward and wrapped her arms around him tightly.

"Mateo!" she cried, her voice trembling with joy. "My son, my son! What a surprise! You are home!"

Mateo held her, confused and overwhelmed. "Mama," he began softly, "I came as fast as I could after receiving the telegram. I am so sorry for our loss… I only wish I could have been here sooner."

His mother pulled back, her brows furrowing. "Loss? What are you talking about?"

Mateo blinked in confusion. "The telegram, Mama. It said that Papa had passed away… that I must come home immediately."

His mother's face turned pale, then a look of astonishment crossed her features. "Telegram? But, hijo, I sent no telegram. Nobody here did! Your father is right here at the back, feeding the chickens!"

Mateo froze. The words struck him like thunder. "Alive?" he whispered, his throat tightening.

"Yes!" she exclaimed, almost laughing now. "Nobody died here. We are all in good health, thanks be to God!"

And as if to prove her words, Mateo's father appeared from behind the house, carrying a basket of chicken feed. His face lit up when he saw his son. "Mateo!" he called out, setting the basket down. "What a blessing! You're home!"

Mateo stood rooted to the ground, trembling. The weight of grief that had crushed him these past days evaporated in an instant, replaced by confusion and disbelief. He staggered forward into his father's embrace, clinging tightly as tears spilled down his cheeks.

His mother placed a hand on his shoulder, still shaking her head. "My son, who would send such a cruel telegram? Who would do such harm to us?"

Mateo could not answer. His heart raced as he tried to make sense of what had just unfolded. Had God deceived him into leaving the monastery? Or was this strange turn yet another act of Divine Providence?

As night settled in, the house was filled with reunion and warmth, but Mateo's soul was troubled. His path had just become even more mysterious.

CHAPTER 27

Back to the Seminary

Questions filled the days following Mateo's shocking return home. His heart rejoiced that his father was alive, yet the mystery of the telegram gnawed at him. Who would go to such lengths to pull him away from the monastery? And for what reason?

He began his investigation quietly, without alarming his parents. First, he went to the small post office in San Agustin and asked about any telegram sent to the monastery. The clerk shuffled through records but found nothing—no log, no receipt, no sender's name. Mateo pressed further, asking if anyone in town had requested the service, but the clerk shook his head. "Brother Mateo, if such a telegram passed through here, it left no trace. It is as though it never existed."

Unwilling to stop, Mateo visited the larger postal office in the nearby town. Again, he found nothing. No record, no signature, no clerk who remembered sending such a message. The officials insisted the telegram may have been sent through some private channel or even forged outside the postal system entirely.

For days, Mateo went from one place to another, questioning neighbors, relatives, and even parish priests, who sometimes helped deliver urgent news. Each inquiry ended in the same blankness: no one knew anything. Whoever had orchestrated this deception had covered his—or their—tracks so well that it was impossible to trace.

Late one evening, while sitting in the silence of his family's small living room, Mateo finally accepted the truth. He would never find out who had lured him away from the monastery with a lie. His heart was heavy with the thought that someone might have wanted to separate him from the Trappists and lead him away from that hidden path. But at the same time, a deeper thought emerged—maybe God Himself allowed this falsehood to redirect him. Divine Providence had always been mysterious in his life.

And so, with resignation, Mateo decided to lay low. For now, there would be no more questions, no more digging. He would return to his studies, uncertain but willing to take the step.

When the day came for him to travel back to the diocesan seminary of San Agustin, Mateo's heart was filled with reluctance. Was this truly the road meant for him? He carried with him both hope and doubt but chose to entrust the journey to God's hands.

The seminary gates were as imposing as ever when he arrived, yet somehow comforting. The familiar stone walls and chapel bell welcomed him back like a long-lost son. He went straight to the office of the Rector.

The Rector, a man of wisdom and kindness, stood as soon as he saw Mateo. "My son!" he exclaimed, embracing him warmly. "You are always welcome here, Mateo. You have been missed."

Tears welled in Mateo's eyes as he knelt to kiss the Rector's hand. "Thank you, Father. I was afraid I might not be accepted again."

"Of course you are," the Rector replied. "You will resume your studies at the beginning of the school year as a third-year Philosophy student. You will now be one year behind your former classmates. You will have a new set of classmates, and I know you can adjust very quickly. Yes, you have missed a year, but do not worry. In two years, you will graduate and then proceed to Theology. God's plan is never late."

Mateo's heart filled with gratitude. "I am deeply thankful, Father. But I must be honest—I cannot depend on my parents for financial support. They are still hesitant about my vocation. I am on my own."

The Rector smiled reassuringly. "Do not fear. There is a very generous organization that has helped countless seminarians who have since become priests. I will recommend you to them."

True to his word, the Rector guided Mateo through the application. Mateo submitted all the necessary requirements, his hands trembling as he signed the papers. Within a few weeks, word came back: he was accepted. A full scholarship would cover his studies until he completed his priesthood formation.

When he read the letter of confirmation, Mateo pressed it against his chest and whispered, "Thank You, Lord." Joy radiated through him like sunlight breaking after a storm.

That same afternoon, Mateo walked through the seminary courtyard, eager yet nervous to see who his new classmates would be and who was still there from the previous year. One seminarian extended his hand to him and introduced himself: "I'm Nick. I will be one of your new classmates." Mateo received Nick's hand with great anticipation and enthusiasm and exclaimed, "I guess we will be spending the next two years together, classmate."

Mateo's heart leapt when he also spotted familiar faces—Emilio, Tomas, and Diego. They were now one year ahead of him, already in their final year of Philosophy.

"Mateo!" Emilio cried, running up to him. Tomas and Diego followed, embracing him tightly.

"We thought you had left us for good!" Diego said with a wide smile.

"And now look—you're back, and just in time," Tomas added. "The seminary isn't the same without you."

Mateo laughed, the sound light and free. For the first time in months, he felt like he belonged again.

But deep inside, he knew the mystery of his path was not yet over.

CHAPTER 28

The Quiet Investigation

Although Mateo attempted to forget about the mystery of the fraudulent telegram, it continued to occupy his thoughts. The image of his father's face, alive and well, juxtaposed with the cruel deception of that false message, haunted his quiet hours of prayer and study. Something in him whispered: the truth must be known.

After weeks of wrestling with his conscience, Mateo resolved to take one more step. This time, he would not rely on his own limited resources. He discreetly sought a reputable private investigator—a man with experience in tracing forgeries, hidden correspondences, and deceptions. Their meeting was quiet, in a small café outside the seminary grounds.

"I need answers," Mateo told him, his voice low. "Whoever sent that telegram wanted to harm me. I cannot focus unless I know the truth."

The investigator nodded, calm and professional. "Leave it to me. Give me whatever information you have, however small, and I will follow the trail."

Mateo handed over what little he had: the date the message arrived, the wording as he remembered it, and the places he had already checked. The investigator listened carefully, then leaned back. "Deception always leaves a trace, even if faint. Trust me, I will find it."

For the first time in months, Mateo felt relief—someone else would carry the burden.

Days passed, filled with the familiar rhythm of seminary life. Mateo attended his Philosophy classes, the lectures on logic and metaphysics stretching his mind once more. In Literature, he saw Fr. Alvarez again. Once, Alvarez had been a regular presence in seminary life, but now he only appeared for his lectures, as he had been fully assigned to the parish. His manner was unchanged: refined, precise, and at times, sharp. Mateo, though respectful, could not help but feel a chill when in his presence, especially now that Alvarez's name lingered in his mind as a possible suspect.

In the music hall, change had also arrived. Fr. Mariano, the new music director, was everything Alvarez was not—gentle, kind, and accommodating. He encouraged the seminarians to lift their voices not only with skill but also with joy. Mateo quickly grew fond of him, sensing a fatherly warmth. It felt like Providence had placed Fr. Mariano there to balance what Mateo quietly endured.

One afternoon, as Mateo was returning from the library, he saw a familiar figure waiting near the seminary gate. It was the investigator. His eyes held a seriousness that made Mateo's pulse quicken.

"I've found something," the man said as they walked to a quiet corner. "The trail is incomplete, but there are leads pointing in two directions. Either the telegram was connected to a woman named Miss Lolita or to Fr. Alvarez. Both had opportunity and motive."

Mateo's breath caught. Miss Lolita—her face appeared vividly in his mind, along with her tangled past of resentment. And Fr. Alvarez—brilliant, influential, but shadowed with ambition.

"Which one?" Mateo asked, almost whispering.

The investigator shook his head. "I cannot yet say. The evidence is not enough to accuse either one. More work must be done. But I warn you—do not pursue the matter yourself. Leave it with me. Concentrate on your studies. In time, I will bring you the truth."

Mateo's heart pounded with both fear and hope. "Very well," he said slowly. "I will wait. But please… be careful."

The investigator gave a slight nod and disappeared into the fading light.

Mateo returned to the seminary chapel that evening and knelt before the crucifix. His whispered prayer trembled on his lips: "Lord, give me patience. Reveal the truth in Your time."

And so, the days continued. Outwardly, Mateo was once again the Philosophy student, the seminarian among his brothers. Inwardly, however, he carried a quiet flame of vigilance, waiting for the final revelation that would one day shake his world again.

CHAPTER 29

The Gruelling Suspicion

The days in the seminary unfolded with quiet order. The bells rang for Lauds before dawn, pulling Mateo and his brothers from their beds into the chapel, where the smell of wax and incense clung to the wooden pews. After prayer came classes—Aristotle and Aquinas in the mornings, pastoral philosophy in the afternoons, and once a week, Literature with Fr. Alvarez.

Outwardly, Mateo moved with discipline, his notes carefully written, his duties completed. He was even cheerful among friends, especially when Emilio, Tomás, and Diego pulled him into lively debates during meals. They teased him about his absence from the seminary the previous year, insisting he owed them stories. Mateo laughed, but his laughter never quite reached his eyes.

Inside, a storm brewed.

Every time he saw Fr. Alvarez enter the classroom with his deliberate, authoritative step, a shiver ran through him. Could it have been him? he asked himself again and again. Yet Alvarez spoke with the same eloquence as before, quoting Dante and Cervantes with passion, even showing flashes of wit. Mateo hated himself for doubting a priest, but the seed of suspicion had been planted, and it took root deeper with each encounter.

When he thought of Miss Lolita, his unease grew heavier. Her bitterness toward him, the venom in her words from the past—they were not easily forgotten. It was easy to imagine her sending that telegram with a cruel smile. And yet, there was no proof, no certainty, only shadows.

At night, when silence filled the dormitory, Mateo lay awake staring at the dark ceiling beams, whispering prayers he once prayed with childlike confidence. Now they trembled with doubt.

"Lord," he whispered, "teach me to trust, even when my heart suspects. Do not let suspicion consume me. And if danger is near, protect me."

One bright Sunday, after Mass, Mateo lingered in the choir loft where Fr. Mariano was rehearsing with some younger seminarians. The music director's gentle manner filled the room with ease.

"You sing well, Mateo," Fr. Mariano said after hearing his voice blend with the others. "But more than skill, I hear longing in your tone. Music reveals what words cannot hide."

Mateo lowered his gaze, surprised. "Longing?"

Fr. Mariano smiled softly. "Yes. For clarity. For peace."

Mateo's chest tightened. How could this man see so deeply so quickly? He gave only a polite smile in return, but Fr. Mariano's words stayed with him long after he left the choir loft.

The investigator had not yet returned with more news, but his earlier words lingered like a shadow: Miss Lolita or Fr. Alvarez. Mateo tried to bury the thought in his books and prayers, but every knock on the seminary door, every unexpected visitor, sent his pulse racing.

And so he lived between two worlds—the ordered routine of study and prayer and the hidden turmoil of suspicion and waiting. The seminary walls kept him safe, but within his heart, a quiet war raged: the war between faith and fear, trust and suspicion.

Mateo knew the truth would come eventually. But he also knew that, until then, he must walk carefully—anchored in God, yet alert to the unseen hand that had already tried once to mislead him.

CHAPTER 30

The Truth Will Come

The summer heat lingered in the cloisters, pressing against the stone walls of the seminary like a heavy cloak. Mateo had just finished Vespers and was returning to his room when a discreet knock came at the side gate. Few visitors came at that hour, but the porter beckoned him urgently.

"Señor Aragon," the porter whispered. "Someone waits for you outside."

It was the investigator. Dressed plainly, his hat pulled low, he carried a small leather satchel that looked heavier than it should. His eyes scanned the courtyard before he spoke.

"I've found something," he said quietly, gesturing for Mateo to walk with him along the outer path near the orchard. The scent of ripe guavas filled the evening air, but Mateo's chest tightened.

The investigator opened his satchel and pulled out a thin bundle of papers. "The telegram was sent from a provincial office. I traced the handwriting on the form—unusual, very neat, but with a certain slant. After comparing it with other documents, I found a strong similarity."

"Similarity with whose handwriting?" Mateo asked, his voice barely steady.

The man hesitated. "A cleric. Someone who has access to both the seminary and the parish."

Mateo froze. His heart pounded in his ears. "Fr. Alvarez?" The words slipped out before he could stop them.

The investigator did not answer immediately. Instead, he handed Mateo a slip of paper: a copy of the telegram, side by side with notes copied from a faculty ledger. The resemblance in the handwriting was striking.

"I cannot conclude with certainty yet," the man finally said. "But the evidence points heavily in his direction. He may not have written it himself, but it bears his mark—or the hand of someone close to him."

Mateo's breath caught. The world seemed to tilt. A priest. A man of God.

"Why would he do this?" Mateo whispered. His hands trembled as he held the papers.

"That," said the investigator, "is what we must discover next. For now, keep this between us. I will continue the trail. There may still be another player involved—someone who wants to remain unseen."

That night, Mateo sat alone in the chapel, staring at the tabernacle's flickering red lamp. His thoughts swirled.

If the suspicion proved true, it was not just betrayal of him—it was betrayal of the Church, of the trust that bound their community together. His heart burned with anger, then collapsed into sorrow.

Kneeling, he buried his face in his hands. "Lord," he prayed, "how do I love Your Church when some of its shepherds may wish me harm? Teach me to separate Your holiness from the weakness of men. Do not let bitterness take root in me."

The silence that followed was deep and heavy, yet within it Mateo felt a whisper, as though God Himself breathed: Persevere. Trust. The truth will come in My time.

From then on, every encounter with Fr. Alvarez was charged with unspoken tension. When the priest lectured on Cervantes the following week, Mateo's mind was not on the text but on the strokes of his handwriting, the tilt of his pen, and the sharpness of his gaze.

The seminary routine continued—prayers, studies, fraternal meals—but beneath its calm surface, Mateo now walked in a world of suspicion, betrayal, and fragile faith.

And he knew the final revelation was drawing closer.

CHAPTER 31

Suspected Conspiracy

The days that followed were a careful dance. Mateo went about his classes, his readings, and his prayers with a veneer of calm, yet beneath the surface, every glance and every interaction was scrutinized. He tried to act as though nothing had happened, but the memory of the telegram and the investigator's initial report was a shadow that stretched across every moment.

A few days later, the investigator returned, arriving unannounced in the seminary courtyard. He looked weary, carrying a thicker satchel than last time.

"Mateo," he said, motioning for him to walk along the hedged path behind the classrooms. "I've followed the trail further. I've discovered some communications, receipts, and notes that point to not just one but possibly two people who may have wanted to destabilize you—Fr. Alvarez and Miss Lolita."

Mateo's stomach tightened. He had expected a lead, but hearing her name sent a fresh chill through him.

The investigator opened his satchel and pulled out several documents. "Notice the timing of these letters and telegrams. They align with when you were away at the monastery. Whoever orchestrated these communications was carefully monitoring your movements, using inside knowledge from someone who had access to your schedules."

Mateo studied the papers, noting the careful handwriting and the deliberate phrasing. He could feel the weight of betrayal pressing down on him.

"I must stress," the investigator continued, "I cannot yet confirm definitively who sent the telegram. But the patterns, the handwriting, and the timing strongly implicate either Fr. Alvarez or Miss Lolita. One may have done it alone, or they may have worked in coordination. Whoever it is, they are cunning and methodical."

Mateo's mind raced. A priest. Someone I once trusted. And… someone I had known for years outside the seminary.

"Do you want me to continue?" the investigator asked. "It will require resources and time. It may even be dangerous if these individuals suspect we are closing in. You will need to step back from your studies to assist me fully."

Mateo shook his head. "No," he said firmly. "I cannot. My studies—my vocation—cannot wait. Whatever the outcome is, I will trust that the truth will come in time. You continue and report back to me when you have the final result."

The investigator nodded, understanding the gravity of the decision. "Very well. But be cautious, Mateo. This is not just about curiosity. It is about your safety and the integrity of your vocation."

That evening, Mateo sat at his desk in the seminary dormitory, the papers spread before him. His thoughts wandered to the monastery, to the silent prayers of the Trappist brothers, and to the music he had shared with them. He missed the quiet, the simplicity, and the unquestioned trust in God's guidance.

Yet here he was, back at San Agustin, surrounded by friends, faculty, and routines—but with a secret that threatened to unravel his peace.

He leaned back, closing his eyes. Lord, guide me. Let me walk this path with courage, without letting suspicion and fear corrupt my heart. Let justice come in Your time, and let me be ready to receive it without bitterness.

Outside, the last rays of the sun touched the spires of the seminary chapel. Mateo picked up his violin, running his fingers over the strings, letting the sound fill the quiet room. The music was both a balm and a reminder—a reminder that even amid uncertainty, there was still beauty, still devotion, still hope.

And somewhere, in the unfolding of events, he felt a quiet reassurance: that no deception, no betrayal, could separate him from his path if he continued to trust in God's Providence.

CHAPTER 32

An Insider Conspirator

Weeks passed in a rhythm of study, prayer, and quiet reflection. Mateo immersed himself in his Philosophy lectures, readings, and discussions with classmates, all the while carrying the weight of the unresolved telegram. The investigation had begun to unfold behind the scenes, but Mateo kept his focus deliberately on his studies, trusting the investigator to follow the trail.

One late afternoon, the investigator returned again, this time with a heavier expression and a thicker folder of documents. Mateo met him discreetly in the quiet garden behind the seminary library, away from the ears of fellow students and faculty.

"Mateo," the investigator began, settling onto the stone bench, "I have additional information for you. I've traced communications and payments that confirm Miss Lolita was not acting alone. She conspired with someone inside the seminary—another seminarian. Someone who also hails from your hometown of San Agustin."

Mateo's heart skipped a beat. A familiar face, someone he might see in the corridors every day, secretly working against him? The thought sent a chill down his spine.

The investigator handed over a series of letters, notes, and receipts. "This seminarian had access to schedules and internal notices, which allowed them to coordinate the fake telegram. Miss Lolita provided the initial plan, and the seminarian executed it from within the seminary."

Mateo took the papers with trembling hands, scanning the handwriting and annotations. His mind tried to connect the dots. It was a betrayal layered in subtlety and careful planning, designed to shake him to his core, and it had worked—if only for a moment—back at the Trappist monastery.

The investigator leaned closer. "I must emphasize, this person is careful and aware of their surroundings. I cannot directly confront them without risking the destruction of evidence. I advise you to focus entirely on your studies and avoid direct involvement for now. Once the investigation is complete, I will report back to you with the final confirmation of the perpetrator's identity."

Mateo nodded, though the unease lingered. "I understand," he said quietly. "I will not interfere. But… thank you for keeping me informed."

That evening, Mateo returned to his dormitory, his footsteps slower than usual. He placed his books on the desk but did not open them. Instead, he leaned back, staring at the ceiling as the weight of the revelation settled in.

A part of him was angry, frustrated that someone he knew, someone he had trusted—even peripherally—had conspired to harm him. Another part of him was deeply grateful for the investigator's diligence, knowing that he would eventually uncover the truth.

Mateo picked up the guitar, letting the first notes fill the room. The music rose in a steady, soothing flow, carrying with it both sorrow and determination. He realized that this challenge, while painful, was also a test of patience, prudence, and faith.

He whispered a silent prayer: Lord, give me the strength to walk this path with integrity. Let me not be consumed by anger nor clouded by suspicion. Let

Your will guide my steps, and let justice, when it comes, be tempered with wisdom.

As the notes lingered in the quiet dormitory, Mateo felt a small measure of peace returning. He could not control the actions of others, but he could control his own response.

And so, he continued his studies, attended his classes, and engaged with his friends, all the while carrying the knowledge that the truth would eventually surface. In the meantime, he would let faith, prayer, and music guide him, even as the shadows of betrayal lingered just beyond the edges of his days.

Chapter 33

Always Remain Calm

The days in the seminary passed with a deceptively calm rhythm. Mateo attended his classes with diligence, studied late into the night, and spent quiet moments at the chapel, letting music and prayer center him. Yet beneath the routine, a tension lingered—unseen, almost imperceptible—like the soft rustle of leaves warning of an approaching storm.

It began with small anomalies. Mateo noticed that some schedules he relied upon—room assignments, notices for study groups—were occasionally misfiled or mysteriously changed. At first, he brushed it off as clerical errors. But over time, the pattern became too deliberate to ignore.

One afternoon, in the philosophy lecture hall, he observed a classmate from another department—the one the investigator had hinted at—glancing repeatedly toward him, then quickly looking away whenever Mateo's eyes met theirs. It was subtle, almost like a silent acknowledgment of something unsaid.

Mateo's mind remained calm. He did not confront the seminarian, nor did he allow the suspicion to consume him. Instead, he noted every detail: the whisper of footsteps behind him in the library, a rearranged book on his desk, and fleeting glances during communal meals. He cataloged it all mentally, letting patience and prudence guide his actions.

Music became his sanctuary. After long hours of study, he would retreat to the music practice room and let the guitar or the piano speak for him. Sometimes he played compositions he had crafted back at the monastery, melodies that carried his longing and his faith. In those notes, he found clarity, as though each chord and cadence reminded him that his path was his own, shaped not by the malice of others, but by his dedication and belief in Divine Providence.

One evening, while walking through the dimly lit corridors, Mateo encountered Fr. Mariano, the new music director. The priest was reviewing the schedule for choir practice. Sensing Mateo's contemplative mood, he offered a gentle smile.

"You've been carrying a lot on your mind, Mateo," Fr. Mariano said softly. "Remember, our challenges often teach us more than our successes ever will. Music, study, prayer… let them be your shield and your guide."

Mateo nodded, grateful for the counsel. "Yes, Father. Thank you."

Though he did not share the details of the investigation, Fr. Mariano's words reinforced Mateo's resolve. He understood that patience and faith were as important as vigilance. The seminarian conspiring against him was clever, but Mateo's integrity and prudence would outlast the fleeting schemes of those driven by envy or malice.

Weeks turned into months. The investigation progressed quietly in the background. Mateo's focus on his studies never wavered. His friendships with Emilio, Tomas, Diego, and his new classmate, Nick, grew stronger. He became known among his peers as someone both kind and disciplined—a young man shaped by the challenges he had faced, yet unbroken by them.

And all the while, the shadow of the seminarian's duplicity remained, subtle but undeniable. Mateo sensed it, cataloged it, but did not act hastily. He knew that truth, like a carefully composed symphony, would reveal itself in time, and when it did, he would meet it with courage and wisdom.

In the meantime, he continued to let music, prayer, and study guide his days. Though the threat lingered, it had not yet touched the core of who he was—a young man determined to walk faithfully on the path he believed God had set before him.

CHAPTER 34

An Outsider's Hand

A discreet note appeared under Mateo's dormitory door several weeks later. It was from the private investigator: a brief message asking him to meet at a quiet café across from the seminary. Mateo, keeping his composure, left his books and walked calmly to the meeting.

The investigator, a sharp-eyed man with a calm demeanor, greeted him and immediately got to the point.

"Mateo, I have the results of my investigation regarding the fraudulent telegram you received at the Trappist monastery," he said, handing Mateo a neatly organized folder. "The evidence points to a conspiracy between Miss Lolita and a seminarian from another department—someone who also hails from San Agustin."

Mateo's eyes narrowed slightly, but his voice remained steady. "Go on."

"The seminarian provided access to internal communications and schedules, enabling Miss Lolita to send the telegram in a way that appeared legitimate," the investigator continued. "Both acted with extreme caution, covering their tracks thoroughly. While I cannot legally confront them without definitive proof, the circumstantial evidence is strong. Whoever orchestrated this act wanted to manipulate your actions, to disorient you, and perhaps even prevent your path toward the monastery."

Mateo's mind raced, yet he remained outwardly calm. The sense of betrayal stung, but he knew that rash anger would solve nothing. Instead, he focused on what the event revealed about human nature—and about himself.

"I see," he said quietly. "Thank you for your thorough work. I need time to process this."

"You'll have it," the investigator replied. "But I suggest you let me handle any next steps. For now, focus on your studies. When the investigation is fully complete, I will report back with everything."

Mateo nodded. He closed the folder and tucked it into his bag. There was relief in knowing the truth, yet he also understood the delicate balance of justice and discretion. His path forward would not be guided by vengeance, but by wisdom and faith.

Back at the seminary, Mateo resumed his studies with renewed focus. Philosophy lectures, literature discussions, and music practice filled his days. He found solace in the rhythm of daily life, in the structure that allowed him to grow without distractions. And though he was aware of the conspiracy that had tried to derail him, he did not let it define him.

Late one evening, in the quiet of his dormitory, he reflected on the events of the past months. From the Trappist monastery to the fraudulent telegram to this investigation—each experience had tested his resolve, his faith, and his discernment. And through it all, he had emerged not bitter, but wiser, more cautious, and more attuned to the ways of Providence.

Mateo picked up the guitar and began to play, letting the music carry the emotions he could not speak aloud. The notes flowed with a mixture of sorrow, hope, and determination—an affirmation that despite deception and treachery, his path remained guided by integrity and faith.

He knew the investigation was not yet fully concluded, but he also knew that he was prepared for whatever revelation might come next. And in that quiet certainty, Mateo felt a sense of peace that no telegram, no scheme, and no betrayal could ever take away.

CHAPTER 35

What's Important

With the investigation behind him and the truth now quietly known, Mateo made the conscious decision to let go. He would not confront Miss Lolita or the seminarian from San Agustin; their intentions, though revealed, were irrelevant to his future. His focus would remain on his studies, on his music, and on cultivating the path God had set before him.

Under the guidance of Fr. Mariano, the seminary's new music director, Mateo quickly became an indispensable part of the choir program. The priest recognized Mateo's natural talent and his disciplined approach to both music and leadership. Mateo assisted in training the seminarians' choir, refining their vocal technique, and arranging pieces for the liturgical calendar.

Word of Mateo's skill began to spread beyond the seminary walls. Invitations came from neighboring schools asking him to judge their choral competitions. Soon, even local government and private organizations sought his expertise for festivals and contests. Mateo approached every assignment with the same diligence he applied to his studies: careful preparation, keen observation, and encouragement for every participant.

Despite his growing reputation, Mateo remained humble. Often, he reminded himself that music was not meant for his own glory, but rather as a gift to nurture and inspire others. He would spend evenings after classes composing small pieces, practicing piano, or helping students polish their performances. "Longing To Be What I Am," his song from his Trappist days, became a personal reminder that music could express the depth of the soul in ways words alone could not.

By the end of the year, Mateo's name was well-known in the musical circles of the region. Schools and seminaries alike recognized him not only as a talented musician but also as a thoughtful judge and mentor. Fr. Mariano often marveled at his growth. "Mateo, you have a gift, and you use it with heart. Keep walking this path, and others will follow in the beauty of your music."

Mateo smiled quietly at the praise, yet he remained focused. Music was both a passion and a mission; every note, every rehearsal, every competition was a step toward fulfilling a larger purpose. He felt the weight of responsibility but also the thrill of opportunity.

Though the shadows of past deception still lingered faintly in his memory, Mateo found peace in knowing he had chosen the right path: one of focus, diligence, and faithful dedication. His life was no longer defined by the schemes of others but by the music he nurtured, the students he guided, and the faith that sustained him.

And so, Mateo's name began to shine—not in scandal or controversy, but in the harmonious blend of talent, perseverance, and the quiet, unassuming power of integrity.

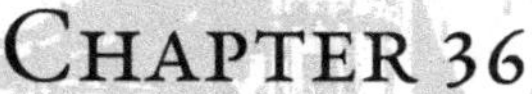

CHAPTER 36

Aiming for Excellence

Mateo's life at the seminary was a delicate balance of discipline, study, and music. Each day began with morning prayers, followed by rigorous classes in Philosophy and Theology, and then afternoons devoted to choir rehearsals and musical mentoring. Despite the growing demands of his musical reputation outside the seminary, Mateo never let his studies falter.

By the end of the school year, the results were undeniable. Mateo had finished his third year of Philosophy not only with flying colors but also earning the Outstanding Academic Excellence Award, a testament to his focus, diligence, and intellectual depth. In addition, he was recognized as the Outstanding

Student of the Year, an honor reflecting both his academic prowess and his exemplary character.

Even amidst these accolades, Mateo remained humble. He often attributed his success to discipline, prayer, and the guidance of his mentors, especially Fr. Mariano, who continued to nurture his musical abilities. Mateo had become a familiar figure in the region's musical circles: schools and organizations sought him as a judge for choral competitions, appreciating not only his expertise but also his fairness and encouragement for the young singers.

His musical influence was growing in parallel with his academic achievements. Mateo's arrangements and guidance elevated choirs from small schools to large institutions, and his reputation as a thoughtful and compassionate mentor spread further. Yet he never let external recognition distract him from his studies or his personal growth.

As the year closed, Mateo reflected on how much he had grown. The challenges of the past—the fraudulent telegram, the near-miss with the Trappist Monastery, and the pressures of being far from home—had all forged in him a resilience that now shone through in both his studies and his music.

He carried the melody of "Longing To Be What I Am" with him as a personal reminder that life, with all its trials and unexpected turns, was a journey of discovering and embracing one's true self. And through it all, Mateo's path was becoming clear: a life dedicated to faith, study, and the transformative power of music.

By the end of the year, Mateo stood on the seminary stage during the awards ceremony, humbly accepting the Outstanding Student of the Year plaque. In his heart, he knew that this was only the beginning—not only of his academic journey but also of his growing influence as a musician and mentor. Every note he played, every student he guided, and every essay he wrote was a testament to his commitment to excellence and his unwavering faith in God's providence.

Mateo had found a rhythm in his life that blended study, music, and spiritual growth. He was learning that success was not only measured in awards and recognition but also in the quiet discipline, the dedication to others, and the joy of pursuing one's gifts to the fullest.

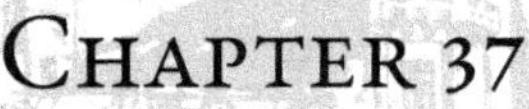

CHAPTER 37

The Senior Year

Mateo stepped into his senior year in the Philosophy department with a renewed sense of purpose. The challenges of the previous years had shaped him into a disciplined student and a skilled musician, and now he was ready to channel all his focus toward academic excellence. His eyes were set on the top honor: Class Valedictorian at the Closing Ceremony twelve months from now. Every lecture, every essay, every discussion would be an opportunity to sharpen his understanding and prepare for the Theology department the following year.

He meticulously planned his schedule: mornings dedicated to lectures and philosophical reflection, afternoons to music, choir practice, and mentoring, and evenings to rigorous study and preparation for examinations. Mateo's peers noticed his determination and quiet intensity, yet he remained approachable, offering guidance to anyone who asked. It was this blend of humility and focus that set him apart, and even at the start of the year, whispers of his potential to achieve the top award floated quietly through the seminary halls.

By the end of the first semester, however, unsettling news swept through the seminary: Fr. Alvarez was returning as the full-time Dean of Studies. Mateo felt a sudden chill. Fr. Alvarez would not just be teaching one subject or visiting occasionally—he would now be living inside the seminary.

Mateo's mind flashed back to the memory that had haunted him since his previous years: the threatening words of Fr. Alvarez, warning him that he would do everything in his power to make Mateo return to the diocesan seminary—specifically under his influence. The reminder sent a shiver down Mateo's spine. He remembered the tone, the calculated coldness, and the unmistakable intent behind those words.

Despite his worry, Mateo knew he had a choice: he could either allow fear and frustration to paralyze him, or he could double down on his goals. He took a deep breath and resolved to focus on his studies, his music, and his spiritual growth, refusing to let Fr. Alvarez derail the careful path he had planned.

Yet the tension lingered, like a shadow at the edge of his daily routine. Each morning, as Mateo entered the classroom or the library, he reminded himself of the reasons he had chosen this path: the love for learning, the desire to serve through faith, and the calling to shape his future according to his convictions.

Mateo's senior year was no longer just a journey of intellectual pursuit—it was a test of resilience, courage, and self-determination. And deep inside, he knew that the months ahead would require more than academic brilliance; they would demand patience, vigilance, and unwavering faith in Divine Providence.

As the semester progressed, Mateo poured himself into his work with even greater determination. Philosophy debates, intricate essays, and mentoring younger seminarians filled his days, but the memory of Fr. Alvarez's looming presence remained a quiet undercurrent, reminding him that true success would require more than intellect—it would require steadfastness of spirit.

And so, Mateo faced the new year with a mixture of excitement and wariness. The top prize of valedictorian, the preparation for Theology, and the challenge posed by Fr. Alvarez were all pieces of a larger journey—one that Mateo intended to navigate with integrity, faith, and resolve.

CHAPTER 38

Calmer and Wiser

Mateo entered his senior year in the Philosophy department with a singular focus: to excel in every aspect of his life at the seminary. More than just academic achievement, he aimed for the Outstanding Student Award, a recognition not only for intellectual brilliance but also for character, leadership, and service. He balanced this pursuit with his ongoing musical responsibilities, determined to leave no part of his calling unattended.

One day, Fr. Mariano asked Mateo to assist him in drafting a letter to the Cardinal, requesting permission for further studies abroad. Mateo approached the task with precision and care, knowing the importance of presenting a clear, respectful, and compelling argument. It was a task that honed his discipline, writing skills, and understanding of Church protocols.

During Fr. Mariano's absence, Fr. Alvarez resumed his role as music director, and Mateo continued as his assistant. This time, however, Mateo approached his duties with wisdom, caution, and restraint, mindful of his words and actions. He carried himself with professionalism, ensuring that all interactions reflected both respect and competence.

Every day, Mateo poured himself into his studies, lectures, and assignments. He participated actively in discussions, helped his peers, and mentored younger seminarians—all while maintaining the rigor required to achieve academic excellence. Mateo's dedication was recognized when he received the Outstanding Academic Excellence award at the end of the year, which was a testament to his intellect and tireless effort.

In addition to academic recognition, Mateo's character, leadership, and integrity were evident to all. His peers admired his humility, diligence, and steadfastness. The student body unanimously voted him as vice president, trusting him to represent their interests, mediate concerns, and help foster a community rooted in cooperation and moral strength.

Amidst these achievements, Mateo remained vigilant. He managed multiple responsibilities with grace, understanding that excellence was not just measured by grades or accolades but by consistency, reliability, and the integrity of his actions. His growth as a scholar, musician, and leader was a visible example to the seminary, inspiring others while strengthening his own resolve.

By the close of the year, Mateo had accomplished more than he had imagined: academic honors, character recognition, and student leadership all in one year. And yet, he remained humble, ever aware that his journey was guided by faith, discipline, and the unseen hand of Divine Providence.

With his sights firmly set on Theology the following year, Mateo had proven to himself—and to the seminary—that dedication, focus, and prudence could navigate even the most challenging circumstances.

CHAPTER 39

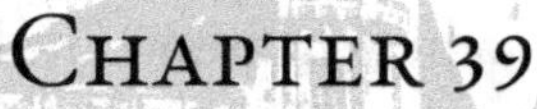

The Graduation

The final year of Philosophy had reached its end, and the closing ceremony loomed on the horizon. It was a moment every seminarian anticipated: the conferring of awards, the recognition of years of discipline, and above all, the celebration of perseverance through trials. For Mateo, it was the culmination of a journey marked by both suffering and triumph, by betrayals endured and victories earned through faith and diligence.

Tradition dictated that the graduating class would sing a special song, a hymn that embodied both gratitude and hope for the future. Fr. Alvarez guided this task for many years, personally composing or arranging the piece and teaching it to the seminarians.

It was considered his hallmark contribution to the seminary's annual rite of passage.

But this year, when Mateo humbly approached him for guidance, Fr. Alvarez turned away with cold indifference.

"Do it yourself," he said with a smirk, his voice dripping with sarcasm. "After all, you're the famous one now. The great conductor. The so-called prodigy everyone talks about. Show them what you've learned."

The words stung not because of the refusal, but because of the tone—a deliberate reminder of the shadow Mateo could never quite escape. It was as if Fr. Alvarez was claiming ownership of Mateo's skills, seeking to remind him who had once trained and molded him.

Mateo did not insist. He bowed his head slightly and walked away. He knew pushing further would only invite ridicule. Instead, he decided to take the challenge upon himself.

That evening, in the quiet of his study, Mateo sat with his notebook open and began to sketch the lyrics of an original graduation song. He reflected on the long nights spent studying, the laughter shared with his classmates, the struggles they had endured together, and the silent prayers that had been whispered over the years. He wanted the song to be a tribute not only to their achievements but also to the bonds that had carried them through.

Line by line, verse by verse, the melody emerged—simple yet profound, carrying both a touch of solemnity and a note of hope. It was not just a song but a testament to resilience, born of rejection yet transformed into creation.

At the same time, Mateo prepared his Valedictory Address, carefully choosing words that would inspire without self-glorification. He wanted his speech to reflect gratitude—for God, for the seminary, for his classmates, and yes, even for the trials that had shaped him.

When the graduating class gathered for choir practice, Mateo explained what had happened.

"Fr. Alvarez will not be teaching us a graduation song this year," he said evenly, without bitterness. "So, we will sing something new—something of our own."

His classmates listened in silence, and then, as he shared the piece he had written, their eyes brightened with enthusiasm. There was pride, too, that one of their own had composed it.

"Mateo," Nick said, "this song… it speaks for all of us."

And so, practice began. The voices rose, tentative at first, then stronger as the melody took root in their hearts. Each rehearsal became not just preparation for the ceremony but a shared experience, binding them closer together. The song became their anthem of farewell, a reflection of the years that had shaped them and the future that awaited beyond the seminary walls.

For Mateo, the dual preparation—song and speech—was exhausting but also exhilarating. He knew the ceremony would not merely be about diplomas and awards. It would be a defining moment: his last act as a Philosophy student, his first as a man standing at the threshold of greater responsibilities.

Despite the lingering shadows and the echoes of condescension in his memory, Mateo chose to respond to insults not with bitterness but by transforming rejection into creation. That decision alone was victory enough.

The following weeks became a whirlwind of rehearsals. Mateo stood before his classmates not as a superior, but as a servant-leader. He guided them through harmonies, adjusting voices with patience, demonstrating parts with clarity, and always encouraging rather than correcting harshly.

Even in the preparation of the graduation program, they did everything themselves. The program design created by Brother Nick was a brilliant proof of his artistic prowess. Mateo and Nick agreed to print on the program the famous quote from one of their favorite books, Khalil Gibran's "The Prophet."

In rehearsals, Mateo emphasized. "Remember, we are not just singing notes. We are giving thanks. Let every phrase be a prayer of gratitude."

The voices of his classmates rose with a strength and beauty that surprised even them. By the final rehearsals, what began as tentative attempts had grown into a sound that was dignified, rich, and deeply moving. It was more than music now—it was their shared legacy, crafted with care and offered in unity.

Finally, the day of graduation arrived.

The seminary hall was filled with guests: families, benefactors, and clergy. The stage was adorned with flowers and banners, and the graduates processed in with solemn dignity, their black cassocks lined neatly, their faces lit with anticipation.

Mateo's eyes scanned the VIP table on stage where the formators sat. He saw Fr. Alvarez among them. The elder priest sat rigid, arms crossed, his face expressionless. When the time came for the graduating class to sing their original song, composed and arranged by Mateo himself, the hall grew still.

The first notes filled the air—soft, reverent, almost like a prayer whispered by many voices at once. Slowly, the harmony expanded, soaring in waves that seemed to lift every heart in the room. Parents wiped tears from their eyes, formators leaned forward in quiet admiration, and classmates sang with a passion born of years of struggle and triumph.

But Mateo noticed something at the VIP table: Fr. Alvarez shifting uncomfortably, restless in his seat, as though the beauty unfolding before him was a weight pressing down. He kept his gaze lowered, pretending indifference, but his fingers tapped the table nervously, betraying what his face refused to show.

When the final chord resolved and the hall erupted in applause, Fr. Alvarez remained still, his hands folded, his expression cold. Yet, for Mateo, that silence was louder than any cheer.

The ceremony moved on. One by one, the awards were announced. Finally, Mateo's name was called for the highest honors: the Academic Excellence Award and the Outstanding Student of the Year Award, as the class Valedictorian. Applause thundered through the hall, his classmates smiling and cheering with genuine joy.

And then, the moment came.

"Ladies and gentlemen," the emcee announced, "we now invite our class valedictorian, Brother Mateo Aragon, to deliver his valedictory address."

Mateo rose, walked with calm composure to the podium, and stood before the assembly. He paused, letting the silence gather. His voice, when he began, was steady and clear.

He thanked his formators, his classmates, his family, and the seminary community. His words carried humility and gratitude, but also a quiet firmness, as though shaped by the trials he had endured. And then, in a sharp yet subtle turn, he quoted words that had long inspired him and his friend Nick, from Kahlil Gibran's The Prophet:

"What was given us here, we shall keep, and if it suffices not, then again must we come together, and together stretch our hands unto the giver."

The hall fell into a hushed reverence. The words lingered in the air like incense, both a reminder and a challenge—that what they had received was precious, but the call to seek more, to give more, would remain with them always.

As Mateo looked out at the assembly, he saw faces moved to reflection, to pride, and even to tears. And though Fr. Alvarez kept his eyes fixed elsewhere, Mateo no longer needed his approval. His journey had taken him beyond that shadow.

The applause that followed was not for brilliance alone, but for a spirit that had chosen gratitude over bitterness, creation over resentment, and excellence over mediocrity.

For Mateo Aragon, it was not only the end of one chapter—it was the beginning of many more.

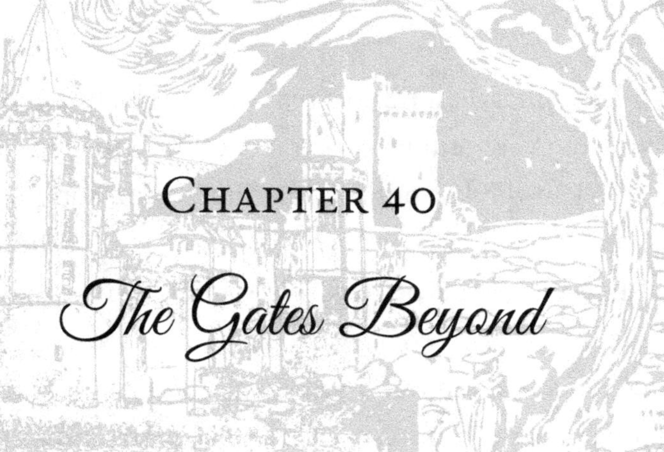

CHAPTER 40

The Gates Beyond

The sun dipped low behind the seminary walls as the echo of applause lingered in the great hall. The ceremony had ended, the awards had been given, and Mateo's voice, steady and composed in his valedictory address, still seemed to reverberate in the hearts of those who heard him. The words of Kahlil Gibran, sharp yet gentle, hung in the air like an invisible benediction:

"What was given us here, we shall keep, and if it suffices not, then again must we come together, and together stretch our hands unto the giver."

For a moment, Mateo had seen a glimmer of recognition flicker across the eyes of his classmates, his professors, and even some of the guests. A reminder that their time together, though ending here, was but the foundation for something greater.

When the last notes of the graduation song faded and the hall emptied into laughter and embraces, Mateo lingered behind. He gathered his folder of speeches, his medal of excellence, and the framed certificate of the Outstanding Student Award. He looked at them briefly—symbols of his triumphs, yes, but also of the weight carried to reach this moment.

Outside, the campus was alive with families and friends. Mateo walked slowly across the familiar courtyard, past the old acacia tree where he once sat as a timid first-year student, unsure if he could ever belong. Now he was leaving as the top of his class, his name etched in the seminary's history not just as a scholar, but as a musician, a leader, and a man tempered by fire.

Yet even in victory, his heart was restless. The road was far from finished. Philosophy had given him structure, clarity, and recognition, but Theology—the deeper ocean—was waiting. He knew it would test not only his mind but also his spirit, his faith, and his very sense of self.

At the gate, Mateo paused. He could hear the faint laughter of his classmates behind him, and further still, the muffled sound of Fr. Alvarez's voice among the faculty. He turned his gaze toward the horizon.

For the first time in years, he felt not fear, not uncertainty, but a quiet strength.

"This is not the end," he whispered to himself. "This is only the beginning."

With diploma in hand and the memory of a song still alive in his chest, Mateo stepped beyond the gates, ready for whatever awaited him in the years to come.

Epilogue

The closing ceremony of the Philosophy Department had ended, but Mateo's journey was far from finished. With medals draped upon him and the echo of his own words still lingering in the auditorium, he walked out into a future marked not by certainty, but by yet another stretch of testing ground.

Theology awaited him. Four more years—each promising heavier responsibilities, more profound questions, and trials that no medal or award could shield him from. Though he carried the honor of being valedictorian and the recognition of his peers and formators, Mateo knew in his heart that these were but reprieves in a life that seemed destined to wrestle with suffering.

Would his struggles ever end? Would the whispers of envy, the shadows of schemes, and the constant weight of proving himself finally relent?

In the quiet of his cell, as the night deepened and the seminary bells tolled, Mateo found himself asking the same question over and over again: Would God ever grant me peace within these walls?

He longed for calm, for a season where his spirit could simply rest in preparation for the vocation he pursued with such devotion. Yet deep down, Mateo sensed that peace would not be given lightly, nor cheaply. His life in the seminary was less a haven than a crucible—shaping, burning, purifying.

And so, with his books stacked neatly at the corner of his desk, his notes prepared for the coming school year, and his eyes staring into the shadows of the night, Mateo whispered a prayer not for ease, but for endurance.

The struggles would continue. The trials would come. But so long as he had breath, Mateo would walk forward—into the uncertainty, into the challenge, into the hope that somewhere along this long, narrow road, God's promise of peace would one day break through.

For now, he remained waiting. Seeking. Believing.

(Concluded in "Checkmate! Mateo")